"Biopunk has been waiting for its William Gibson, to bring a whole new vision of the future as Mr. Gibson did for cyberpunk, and Daniel Suarez has done it. . . . Exhilarating, alarming—Daniel Suarez plays the two great thrills of sci-fi against each other, and not just for fun. He thinks this is coming, and he means it. Read it and wonder."
—*The Wall Street Journal*

"Besides being a rockin' thriller, *Change Agent* is a vivid depiction of where ubiquitous gene editing might take us. I came away believing I'll be less surprised by the future."
—Kevin Kelly, senior maverick for *Wired* and *New York Times* bestselling author of *The Inevitable*

"The depth and sophistication of Suarez's dystopian world—not to mention his facility at making complex science intelligible to the nonexpert—rivals anything Michael Crichton ever did."
—*Publishers Weekly* (starred review)

"The action scenes are plenty lively, [but] the best thing about the book is its depiction of a troublesome future in which people can change physical identities the way they change clothes. . . . A natural at making future shocks seem perfectly believable, Suarez delivers his most entertaining high-tech thriller yet."
—*Kirkus Reviews*

"The ultimate form of identity theft is just a genetic edit away in Suarez's newest fast-paced, speculative thriller. . . . Offer this to Michael Crichton and science fiction–suspense fans."
—*Booklist*

Praise for
Daniel Suarez

"*Daemon* does for surfing the web what *Jaws* did for swimming in the ocean. . . . Both entertaining and credible. . . . An impressive debut novel."
                                              —*Chicago Sun-Times*

"A chilling yet entirely plausible story of technology gone awry."
                                  —*Tampa Bay Times* on *Daemon*

"Fiendishly clever. . . . An almost perfect guilty-pleasure novel."
                        —*The Dallas Morning News* on *Daemon*

"A riveting debut."   —*Publishers Weekly* on *Daemon* (starred review)

"This thrill-a-nanosecond novel is certainly faithful to the techno-traditions of Michael Crichton and should delight not only readers of the 'science gone awry' genre, but general adventure readers as well."
                                       —*Booklist* on *Daemon*

"Suarez's not-just-for-gamers debut is a stunner."
                              —*Kirkus Reviews* on *Daemon*

"Greatest. Technothriller. Period. Suarez presents a fascinating account of autonomous logic-based terrorism, incorporating current and antici-pated technologies to create a credible and quite clever story."
         —William O'Brien, former director of cybersecurity and comm-
                  unications policy for the White House on *Daemon*

"*Daemon* is the real deal—a scary look at what can go wrong as we depend increasingly on computer networks."
                   —Craig Newmark, founder of Craigslist on *Daemon*

"*Freedom*™ surpasses its smart, exciting predecessor. This concluding volume crackles with electrifying action scenes and bristles with intriguing ideas about a frightening, near-future world. The two books combined form the cyberthriller against which all others will be measured."
—*Publishers Weekly* (starred review)

"Suarez continues his popular technothriller. . . . *Daemon* fans will be pleased with the exciting conclusion."   —*Booklist* on *Freedom*™

"An engrossing, fast-paced tale of speculative fiction."
—SFSite.com on *Freedom*™

"You'll hear a lot of reviewers compare Suarez to [Michael] Crichton, including me for his previous book *Kill Decision*. And Suarez deserved the honor in the truest sense . . . he had achieved a truly Crichton-level of storytelling. But with *Influx*, Suarez becomes the master, and Crichton is the one who is honored by the comparison."
—Stephen L. Macknik, *Scientific American*

"*Influx* is done with the dazzling sophistication, the play of ideas, the hints of a new understanding almost within our grasp that characterize sci-fi in the cybertronic age."   —*The Wall Street Journal*

"With this terrifying thriller, Suarez provides further support for the proposition that he's a worthy successor to the late Michael Crichton. . . . Suarez once again mixes science and fiction perfectly."
—*Publishers Weekly* on *Influx* (starred review)

"The characters (even the not-strictly-human ones) are vivid, the pacing is perfect, the villain is capital-E evil, and the author's near-future world is so well developed that you completely buy even his wildest speculations. A magnificent tour de force."   —*Booklist* on *Influx*

"*Influx* is dark . . . it's fun . . . and it's a thinker. Just what I've come to expect from Daniel Suarez."   —GeekDad.com

"*Influx* as a whole is riveting. Fans of science fiction and thrillers will enjoy this engrossing combination of both genres." —Shelf Awareness

"It's a delicate balance, but one that Suarez manages with the skill and audacity of Philippe Petit. Don't know that name? Petit is the only tightrope walker ever to cross between the Twin Towers. Like the daring Frenchman, Suarez goes higher and takes bigger risks than many of his contemporaries or predecessors. It's a technique which allows and enables his work to stand out." —SFSite.com on *Influx*

"*Kill Decision* really nails it . . . Daniel—wow—awesome." —Brad Feld, Business Insider

"Perfectly blending nail-biting suspense with accessible science, bestseller Suarez (*Daemon*) establishes himself as a legitimate heir to Michael Crichton with this gripping present-day thriller." —*Publishers Weekly* on *Kill Decision* (starred review)

"This is the kind of mind-expanding novel that uses entertainment to make powerful, important points about alarming current trends; the novel as cautionary tale has rarely been better executed. . . . Highly recommended." —Tim O'Reilly on *Kill Decision*

"*Kill Decision* reads like a Michael Crichton thriller." —Associated Press

"A confident thriller that leaves us wondering not whether its fictional premise will one day become reality, but when." —*Kirkus Reviews* on *Kill Decision*

ALSO BY DANIEL SUAREZ

Daemon

Freedom™

Kill Decision

Influx

CHANGE AGENT

Daniel Suarez

DUTTON

DUTTON

An imprint of Penguin Random House LLC
375 Hudson Street
New York, New York 10014

Previously published as a Dutton hardcover, April 2017

First paperback printing, April 2018

Copyright © 2017 by Daniel Suarez
Penguin supports copyright. Copyright fuels creativity, encourages diverse voices, promotes free speech, and creates a vibrant culture. Thank you for buying an authorized edition of this book and for complying with copyright laws by not reproducing, scanning, or distributing any part of it in any form without permission. You are supporting writers and allowing Penguin to continue to publish books for every reader.

DUTTON and the D colophon are registered trademarks of Penguin Random House LLC.

The Library of Congress has catalogued the hardcover of this book as follows:

Names: Suarez, Daniel, 1964– author.
Title: Change agent : a novel / Daniel Suarez.
Description: New York : Dutton, [2017]
Identifiers: LCCN 2016030244| ISBN 9781101984666 (hardcover) |
ISBN 9781101984680 (ebook) | 9781101984673 (trade paperback)
Subjects: LCSH: International Criminal Police Organization—Fiction. |
Genetic engineering—Fiction. | BISAC: FICTION / Technological. | FICTION
/ Science Fiction / Adventure. | GSAFD: Science fiction.
Classification: LCC PS3619.U327 C48 2017 | DDC 813/.6—dc23 LC record available
at https://lccn.loc.gov/2016030244

-

Printed in the United States of America

1 3 5 7 9 10 8 6 4 2

Book Design by Amy Hill

This book is a work of fiction. Names, characters, places, and incidents either are the product of the author's imagination or are used fictitiously, and any resemblance to actual persons, living or dead, business establishments, events, or locales is entirely coincidental.

For my mother, Jane Haisser.
You will always be my hero.

Full fathom five thy father lies.
Of his bones are coral made.
Those are pearls that were his eyes.
Nothing of him that doth fade,
But doth suffer a sea-change
Into something rich and strange.

—*The Tempest,*
William Shakespeare

Chapter 1

Before we begin, have you any questions about genetic editing, Mr. and Mrs. Cherian?" The counselor took a whopping bite from a vada pav sandwich as he clicked through their file.

The young Mumbai couple exchanged uncertain looks. In their late twenties, well-groomed, and dressed in crisp business casual clothes, they appeared a step above the cramped, dingy, and windowless office around them. Nonetheless here they were. The wife appeared especially ill at ease.

The husband shook his head. "No questions at the moment, no." He looked to his wife reassuringly. Patted her on the knee.

She spoke up. "How does the procedure work?"

The counselor answered with his mouth full. "Ah, an inquiring mind." She narrowed her eyes at him.

The husband cut in. "My wife and I are *both* attorneys. Given the legal status of this enterprise, we were understandably reluctant to research the topic on our own devices."

"Well then . . ." The counselor finished chewing and wiped his fingers on a crumpled napkin. "I have something that should address your questions." He noisily rooted around in his desk drawer and in a moment produced a device the size and shape of a paperback book, which he placed on the cluttered desktop between them. When he pressed down on the device it unfolded into a pylon shape—sporting several lenses facing forward and back. It booted up, white light glowing within.

The wife drew stylish mirror glasses from her purse and donned them to shield her eyes. "A *glim*? You think we'd allow you access to our retinas? This is out—"

"No retinal scanning, I assure you, Mrs. Cherian. Merely a brief in-eye presentation."

The husband looked to his wife. "They have our DNA, love. Retinas are the least of it."

"Neelo, I want our embryo transferred back to the clinic."

"My love, we—"

"This place is a rat hole. A defunct export office by the look of it."

"All part of the disguise, Mrs. Cherian. We must not attract undue attention from the authorities. But rest assured, our labs are well funded—run by the largest genediting syndicate in the world, Trefoil. None are more sophisticated."

"My love, remember: they came highly recommended."

She grabbed her bag as if to go. "Neelo, we are law-abiding people."

"We've discussed this, cherub. Principled positions are admirable, but other parents are doing this. We as well must do everything we can to prepare our son for the world in which he will live." He gestured to the glim on the table. "Why don't we watch the presentation and see how we feel afterward?"

She sighed—and reluctantly removed her mirror glasses.

The counselor beamed. "Very good. Please look forward. It will find your retinas in a jiffy."

In a moment, from their perspective, the air above the desk filled with a highly detailed 3D model of the double helix of DNA. It rotated there, an utterly convincing virtual object—seemingly as real as the desk. Yet the floating DNA existed only as a rich, plenoptic light field projected directly onto their retinas and unseen by anyone not targeted by the glim.

Light field projectors like these had largely replaced physical televisions, computer screens, and mobile OLED displays in the last decade or so. Beaming imagery directly onto a viewer's retinas instead of spraying photons all over the place had many advantages—authentic augmented reality being one. Environmental sustainability another. Privacy another still.

A female narrator's voice came to them via a focused acoustic beam. *"Initially developed in 2012, CRISPR technology is a search-and-replace tool for modifying DNA—the blueprint of all living things."*

The word "CRISPR" appeared with the letters expanding into full words in turn.

"Shorthand for 'clustered regularly interspaced short palindromic repeats,' CRISPR derives from a naturally occurring process in bacterial immune systems—and it has been adapted by modern science to permit targeted genetic edits of plant, animal, and human embryos."

The 3D animation showed a labeled RNA molecule enter the scene.

"The process begins by seeding a 'guide RNA' with both a target and a payload genetic sequence . . ."

Labels identified them in turn as they were inserted into the RNA molecule.

"This guide RNA is then injected into an embryonic cell's nucleus . . ."

The RNA clamped onto the double helix of DNA, unzipping it.

". . . where it reads the embryo's DNA. Wherever a match for the target sequence is found . . ."

The 3D image highlighted a match between the RNA target sequence and a segment of the cell's DNA.

". . . a natural cutting protein acts as a molecular scalpel, severing the DNA chain . . ."

The animation showed the double helix of DNA cut.

". . . removing the matching segment . . ."

The animation showed it being removed.

". . . and inserting a copy of the payload DNA in its place."

The RNA's payload sequence copied itself into the gap, and the DNA quickly rejoined.

"In this way human embryos may be safely and reliably 'edited' in vitro to correct deadly heritable genetic disorders."

Moving music swelled as the scene dissolved to a life-sized 3D projection of a beautiful but despondent little African girl with cloudy blind eyes. She looked as real as if she sat in the room with them.

"CRISPR-developed cures for cystic fibrosis, muscular dystrophy, sickle-cell anemia, Huntington's disease, hemophilia, and more have

already saved or improved the lives of hundreds of millions of people world-wide . . ."

The scene dissolved into a new image—one of the now smiling girl with clear brown eyes, reaching up to smudge flour onto her mother's nose. They both laughed and embraced as they made cookies together.

"Ending a legacy of suffering and for the first time putting humanity in control of its own genetics."

The image tilted skyward to show a brightly lit horizon. A new dawn.

"Theoretically there is no limit to the desirable edits CRISPR can perform."

Dark clouds moved in, obscuring this glowing horizon. Ominous music rumbled.

"However, international law currently prohibits edits beyond those designed to correct a short UN-approved list of genetic disorders. Despite this, our expert researchers have perfected hundreds of highly beneficial CRISPR edits. Edits that increase both the quality and the quantity of human life."

The music rose as the image ascended, finally bursting through the gray cloud layer into an endless expanse of sunlight beyond. No horizon in sight.

"And unlike other gene therapies, CRISPR edits are heritable— meaning they will be passed down to all future generations of your family line—what's known as 'germ line engineering.' This means your investment today will pay rich dividends for all your child's descendants."

The scene transitioned to a life-sized and utterly realistic projection of a healthy five-year-old South Asian boy, who rotated slowly before them.

"For example, a minor edit to a human embryo's DAF2 gene could add thirty healthy years to a child's life. A change to BCAT1 could add even more."

The image of the boy aged to an adult and then beyond until he had a full shock of gray hair—but an otherwise healthy frame. He lifted up a laughing grandchild with ease as they ran toward a zoo exhibit.

The imagery then dissolved to show a young man, studious and attentive in a classroom.

"A change to gene DLG3 can improve memory, while a series of edits within the M1 and M3 gene clusters can substantially increase intelligence."

The image morphed to the teen wearing a valedictorian cap and gown. He smiled as he took the podium amid applause, ostensibly to address his graduating class.

The imagery shifted to an athletic young woman running on a track against several close competitors.

"A tweak to the MEF2 gene can bestow type II 'fast-twitch' muscle fibers . . ."

The young woman outpaced the other sprinters, raising her arms as she burst through the finish tape to cheers.

". . . increasing physical prowess."

The imagery resolved again to a double helix of DNA, with segments snipped and replaced here, there, and elsewhere.

"Other even more exciting edits are being developed to meet the demands of our increasingly competitive world. Be sure to ask your genetic counselor for a full list of edits in your price range. No matter which you choose, you'll be giving your child a timeless gift, one that they will be able to pass down to their own children—the first truly priceless family heirloom."

The DNA looped as the image zoomed out to soft, inspiring music, transforming into a three-cornered continuous shape.

Text appeared above and below the logo as it pulsed with life:

TREFOIL LABS

Evolution by design.

Moments later the virtual logo blinked out of existence as the counselor pressed down on the glim to fold it. He scooped the glim back into his desk drawer. "I trust that answered your questions."

The husband and wife both looked somewhat dazed at the sudden disappearance of the alternate reality.

The wife was first to recover. "Could such edits be done on an adult person?"

The counselor laughed, putting his sandwich down and clasping his hands. "Now that would be valuable indeed! But alas, no, Mrs. Cherian. Editing the DNA of one cell out of thirty-five trillion would not accomplish much. That's why these changes need to be made while your child is but a zygote—a single fertilized cell."

She nodded to herself. "I see."

"You and I will remain as we are, but your child has no such limitation." He studied her expression, pausing with the experienced cadence of a true salesman. "Shall we discuss the desired edits for your future son?"

The husband took his wife's hand. "Are you ready to proceed, my love?"

She visibly struggled with powerful emotions.

The counselor had seen it before. "Mrs. Cherian, all creatures select genetic preferences when they choose a mate. But science now gives you and your husband the ability to adjust your child's genetics just a bit further—*together.*"

The husband again placed his hand on her knee.

She shook her head. "It seems against Nature."

The counselor spoke softly. "This is the very same process Nature follows to eliminate viral DNA in bacteria. The same process used under the UN's Treaty on Genetic Modification."

"Yes, but to cure deadly genetic defects, not to tailor-make a child."

The husband shook his head. "We are not tailoring our child. We are correcting genetic weaknesses. Is not a weak memory fatal to a future doctor or attorney?"

"Where does this sort of thinking lead us, Neelo—eugenics?"

The counselor shook his head slowly. "No, no, Mrs. Cherian. There are three billion letters in the human genome. Most people edit six to twelve—minor edits indeed."

"Remember, love, what did you say when you saw the Persauds' little boy? Is that not why we are here?"

She fell silent.

The husband turned to the counselor. "We don't want many edits, of course."

"Nor would you need them, Mr. Cherian." He started tapping at an unseen screen. "But even minor edits can go a long way to help your child in a rapidly evolving world. Some edits are more costly than others, of course, but who can put a price on parental love?"

The husband studied his wife, who was literally wringing her hands, but he spoke to the counselor. "Which edits would you recommend?"

"I always suggest the DAF2 edit. Why not start your child out with up to three decades more of healthy living? So they can be there in your twilight years." The counselor made some entries on the invisible screen. "How could such a thing be wrong?"

The Cherians exchanged appraising looks.

"Longer life, of course, suggests related edits—LRP5 for extra strong bones, PCSK9 for a greatly reduced risk of heart disease . . ." He clicked unseen UIs.

"The next question is whether you prize intellectual excellence over physical prowess. Heightened intellect requires more complex edits— and is, thus, more costly. You can choose both, of course, budget permitting." He looked up at the parents.

They stared, frozen by the magnitude of the decision.

"Well, let us see what the Greek ideal—body and mind—would require." The counselor displayed the price to them.

"That's more than a year of university, Neelo."

"But with these edits our boy could very well win a full scholarship."

"I am uncomfortable with this."

"Why? Because some government bureaucrat says it's not allowed? Do you really think the wealthiest families are not doing this, my love?"

She sighed and looked away.

He took her hand again. "We must do it. For our son's sake—no matter how uncomfortable it makes us."

Just then they heard a *BOOM* that caused them all to jump in their seats.

The wife turned. "What was that?"

The counselor was already clicking away at invisible screens. "Oh, my . . . Mr. and Mrs. Cherian, please . . . a moment."

The wife grabbed her husband's arm. "What was that, Neelo?"

The husband stood as the counselor did. The sound of running feet and muffled shouts came from the hall. "Speak up, man!"

The counselor motioned for calm. "It would appear that the Brihan-mumbai are raiding this facility."

"The police?"

"Do not be alarmed. We have made contributions to the appropriate authorities. This is clearly a mix-up. In any event, we have numerous concealed exits for just such a contingency." He gestured to his office doorway. "If you would please follow me . . ."

The counselor moved quickly out his office door and into a narrow corridor, which was quickly crowding with other couples and their counselors. Some clients shielded their faces from one another with handbags and scarves.

The husband clasped his wife's hand and followed closely. "This is outrageous."

"What about our embryo, Neelo?"

The counselor glanced backward. "Not to worry, folks. As I said, we'll get this mix-up sorted."

Someone shouted in alarm behind them. The Cherians looked back to see the door at the far end of the hallway kicked in. Police in black body armor poured through, shouting, "*Zameen par sab log!*"

Someone screamed and the crowd of clients stampeded.

A lab security guard emerged from a side door—pistol in hand.

The police shouted it in unison, "*Bandook! Bandook!*"—red laser dots clustering on the guard's chest as he stood slack-jawed. Deafening POPS filled the corridor. Screaming as everyone scattered. The security guard dropped like a bag of cement.

The husband pulled his wife down to the floor alongside him. "Down, love! Get down!"

People ran past them in a panic toward an unseen rear exit—some trampling the husband and wife as he shielded her. "Watch it, damn you!"

The police shouted again, *"Zameen par sab log!"*

Their counselor was nowhere to be seen. The husband spoke into his wife's ear. "We must say nothing until we've seen counsel, love. I need to phone Anish."

His wife was silent.

The husband noticed blood on his hand. Panicked, he padded his sides down. "My love, I . . ." And then, finding nothing, he looked to his wife.

A small bullet hole pierced her temple.

"No . . ." He cupped her head. Blood pooled beneath them both, expanding quickly across the cheap, dirty carpet.

He tried to form words—then finally screamed in horror as police approached behind him, guns raised. "No! No!"

He hugged her body close, shrieking in anguish.

The helmeted and armored police tried to pull him from her, but he would not let go.

"My love. No, my love!"

Chapter 2

C **hange comes. Inexorable.** Most times it arrives gradually—but sometimes change is an earthquake. Cherished assumptions crack. Rocks of stability crumble. Chasms of experience open between adjacent generations.

Thinking back on his childhood, Kenneth Durand remembered his millennial parents enduring their own technological earthquake—the disruption of every industry. Their college degrees useless and their student debt insurmountable, they fell, like many others, out of the middle class. His father's ready smile was replaced by a mask of worry that remained until the day he died. Automation and disintermediation rocked their world.

And everyone thought that was big change.

It was nothing—just a tremor.

Two even larger shock waves came for Durand's generation.

The first was mass adoption of light fields. Suddenly what you saw with your own eyes wasn't necessarily reality. Most of the consumer electronics industry disappeared.

The second and *far* more disruptive shock wave was the fourth industrial revolution: synthetic biology. What was once manufactured was now increasingly grown by custom-designed organisms—algae, yeasts, bacteria. Automobile bodies grown from chitin. Biofuels from custom *E. coli* bacteria. Deathless meat and cultured dairy products from sustainable cellular agriculture. *Biofacturing* instead of manufacturing. Life itself harnessed to the human will.

Societies that incorporated these advances moved on. Those that could not did not. Instead, they languished in the debt, political paralysis, and recriminations of the previous age.

Durand had made his own choice, and the memory of those he'd left behind still ached. No doubt migrants of prior eras had always suffered the same anguish. They saw a brighter future somewhere and someway else and walked the difficult path that led them there. He'd disappointed so many people. Violated beloved traditions of service and loyalty. But life was all about difficult choices.

Durand contemplated headlights from eighty stories above as the first light of dawn crested the Johor Strait. Singapore's robot rush hour was already under way far below. Autonomous electric cars packed the expressways, their LED headlights coursing over the landscape like rivers of white-hot lava.

He barely paid attention to the voice of a female newscaster in his ear, "... *Korea prepares to celebrate the anniversary of its reunification, Seoul officials are rolling out the red carpet for Chinese dignitaries—honoring Beijing's pivotal role in the nearly bloodless coup and invasion that deposed the Pyongyang regime . . .*"

From the traffic patterns below, it was clear humans were no longer behind the wheel. No stopping and starting, but traffic flowing smoothly, closely coordinated, optimized.

"Mathematics on parade," his father had called it. Each vehicle informed by its neighbors, and by the whole. These days you couldn't drive yourself to work even if you wanted to. Manual driving was prohibited on the expressways. Humans could not keep pace.

That was something his father well knew.

Mathematics on parade. An experienced and talented civil engineer, his father spent the last ten years of his life getting downsized from entry-level retail jobs. He died of a heart attack while Durand was still in high school—leaving them in poverty.

The anchorwoman's voice continued in his ear: "*The Australian Coast Guard rescued passengers of a so-called zombie ship adrift off the Port Arthur coastline on Tuesday. Packed with hundreds of desperate migrants, the vessel had been abandoned without food or water after traffickers reportedly received payment to ferry the refugees to Indonesia, where they were told jobs awaited."*

Durand turned away from the skyline and back to the high-rise jogging path. A glance at stats glowing in the corner of his vision showed he still had a chance to maintain a seven-minute mile.

He resumed jogging as the news continued.

"Fleeing climate-change-related crop failures, civil war, and rising ocean levels, tens of millions of desperate migrants are on the move in what has become the largest sustained migration in human history . . ."

Durand's LFP glasses tinted against the glare of dawn. The tropical humidity was already bearing down. He jogged through fogs of atomized water that cooled him at intervals. The track arced rightward on a five-kilometer loop traversing the top of the Hanging Gardens residential complex. Lush jungle plants lined the inner edge.

Durand pushed himself harder, curving along the path. Fashioned of spongy metamaterial, the surface reduced the impact on his joints. An infinity pool ran along the outer edge, and he jogged past a swimmer in goggles and a water cap. A lush garden path ran below and beyond that—near the outer railing. Everything in sight had been meticulously designed—what urban planners had taken to calling "the built environment."

"The International Olympic Committee gathers in Tokyo this week to debate the coming generation of genetically altered athletes. At issue is whether CRISPR edits should disqualify competitors for participation in Olympic and professional sport. At present, no reliable test exists to reveal embryonic genetic edits, potentially putting in peril long-standing records of human physical achievement."

As he ran, Durand focused on the ubiquitous construction cranes studding the Singapore skyline. Two-hundred-story buildings were going up all over the CBD. Mute testimony that the boom was on.

It was difficult to pinpoint the year Singapore became the technology capital of the world. Economists usually placed that somewhere between ratification of the UN Treaty on Genetic Modification and the second wave of moon landings. But certainly by the dawn of the Gene Revolution, the technological crown had shifted from America.

Silicon Valley did not go quietly.

Palo Alto, Mountain View, Cupertino, and San Francisco ran through all the Kübler-Ross stages of economic grief. Applied billions in defibrillating tax breaks to jump-start investment. Held embarrassing VR publicity stunts. In the end the US government was practically giving away H-1B visas.

But nothing could stop the exodus. The Valley was done. Synthetic biology finished it—though, to be fair, that wasn't the Valley's fault.

Synthetic biology was the transistor of the twenty-first century. Yet political realities in America made it increasingly unfeasible for entrepreneurs there to tinker with the building blocks of life. Every cluster of human cells was viewed as a baby in America. A quarter of the population wasn't vaccinated. A majority of Americans didn't believe in evolution. Social-media-powered opinions carried more influence than peer-reviewed scientific research. In this virulently anti-science atmosphere, synbio research was hounded offshore before it had really begun. Activists crowed over their victory.

The rest of the world did not let the opportunity pass it by.

By then, Silicon Valley's forte—circuitry and software—had become cheap global commodities, created everywhere. Network-centric economic disruption was largely complete. Every nook and cranny of modern life had already been disintermediated. The gig economy and time-share rentals had cannibalized the US consumer base, low-bidding the middle class out of existence. It was what had done Durand's parents in. He still remembered them huddled in one room of their home, while debt-collection software rented out the rest of their house over the Internet.

The world moved on, hungering for answers to the pressing problems of a rapidly heating world. Looking for ways to feed the hundreds of millions of people rendered jobless by automation, skyrocketing global debt, climate shifts, and war.

Synthetic biology delivered—engineering yeasts, algae, and bacteria as the machinery of sustainable production. Growing and evolving integrated biofactory systems. Serving as a foundry for new pharmaceuticals and CRISPR-edited climate-change-resistant crops—like C4 photosynthesis rice—to feed earth's ten billion people. Built environments where cyanobacteria converted light into sugar and custom *E. coli* converted sugar into biofuel—organisms altered to feed into each other's processing loops. Bespoke *E. coli* that scrubbed the oceans of pollutants or sequestered carbon.

Innovations in xenobiology allowed for the wholesale expansion of the biological alphabet itself: xenonucleic acids (XNA) such as HNA, TNA, GNA, LNA, and PNA—sugars not utilized in the natural world that could create entirely new cellular machinery and compounds that did not interact with natural biological systems—launched entire industries in biological computing and bio blockchain tech.

Life itself had become the next systems architecture. And it was hard to argue with its accumulated uptime.

And so the Valley moved overseas, as did many of the people and firms in it, reconvening in a locale more receptive to science—if not quite liberal democracy. By the mid-2030s most synbio start-ups were Changi-bound. Within a decade, new trillion-dollar companies called Singapore home, replacing oil and finance as the main industries in the tiny island republic. And it had yet again transformed the city-state's skyline.

Durand noticed a line of urban farming towers in the distance. A hundred stories each and draped in vines, the dozen towers resembled overgrown postapocalyptic ruins—except for their glittering organometallic lights. Acre for acre, the towers produced ten times the food of a traditional farm on just a fraction of the water. Zero pesticides. Almost entirely automated.

Nearby stood "pharm" towers, whose crops had been genetically modified to produce pharmaceutical compounds.

Beyond the towers clouds of commercial drone traffic surged past on the aerial logistics highway wrapping the northern and eastern shores—headed toward Changi and the aerial interchange that fed into the CBD. Silhouetted against the glowing eastern horizon, the delivery drones resembled flocks of birds.

Durand's newsfeed went to commercial—an American man talking fast: "*. . . the premier IGEA-certified provider for all custom cell-cloning* *services, gene synthesis, subcloning, mutagenesis, bespoke promutagens, variant libraries, and vector-shuttling services. cDNA clones available in your preferred vector . . ."*

No skipping or muting commercials; they'd be there waiting for you next time. Better to let them play. Besides, his lap was nearly finished.

Durand ran between rows of bioluminescent trees on the rooftop approach to Tower Six. The soft glow from the trees had begun to dim as the first rays of sunlight touched their broad leaves. Engineered like everything else around him, the plants were as beautiful as they were functional, illuminating roads and sidewalks throughout Singapore.

He sprinted the last twenty meters, pushing with everything he had. The building security system recognized him, and glass doors silently opened, as he knew they would. Durand slowed to a stop as he entered the blessed cool of the rooftop lobby.

The tower's synthetic female voice spoke in Asian-accented English: *"Good morning, Mr. Durand. I trust you had a pleasant exercise."*

Durand ignored the voice. He knew it was just a narrow AI. Any input he granted it would be stored for later use or misuse, nothing more. It did not "care" about him any more than his soap dish did. Instead he checked his running time while he caught his breath and stretched.

The newsfeed resumed in his ear: *"Attorney and internationally acclaimed human rights activist Kamala Cherian was slain Tuesday evening in a botched police raid on a black market CRISPR lab in the Kurla district of Mumbai . . ."*

Durand stopped cold.

"Indian authorities claim Ms. Cherian, a client of the facility, was caught in the cross fire between police and lab security. Cherian's death will likely only increase public opposition to armed raids on illicit genetic editing labs under a mandate by the UN Treaty on Genetic Modification. Ratified in 2038, the agreement was intended to halt the global spread of unregulated genetic editing of human embryos."

Durand spoke to the newscaster. "Britney. Pause news."

The synthetic anchorwoman answered. *"Pausing news."*

He pondered the information for several moments. "Britney, phone Michael Yi Ji-chang."

The synthetic anchorwoman, now his assistant, replied, *"I'm ringing Detective Sergeant Michael Yi Ji-chang. One moment . . ."* A pause. *"I have Sergeant Yi Ji-chang on an encrypted line."*

A man's voice answered. He had a slight Korean accent. *"A call this early can't be good."*

"Tell me about the Mumbai raid."

"What's to tell? Trigger-happy cop killed a VIP."

"Does Claire know yet?"

"Yes, and I'll tell you what I told her: we shouldn't overreact."

"The Brihanmumbai were supposed to raid the lab—not the clinic. There wouldn't be civilians in the lab. Now an innocent woman is dead."

"Not entirely innocent."

"Come on, Mike."

"If she had obeyed the law, Ms. Cherian would still be alive. Would you rather a cop died?"

"Of course not, but that's not the choice."

"Look, we just provide the intel. National police conduct the raids. It's not on us."

"Bullshit. We have leverage over the NCBs. We should only share lab locations with them."

"If we expect full reciprocity, Interpol needs to provide national police with the ability to follow the money into these syndicates—to get to the kingpins. That means your whole link analysis."

Durand felt a familiar fear. "Do you remember what we said after Djibouti?"

"This isn't misuse of intelligence, Ken."

"Do you remember?"

"This was a mistake—and not even our mistake."

"The media is making these raids out as murdering hopeful parents. You and I both know what happens if the public turns against the Genetic Crime Division."

"Twenty years from now, when kids have hands growing out of their foreheads, the public will want to know why the hell we didn't do something to shut these illegal labs down."

"Agreed, so let's defuse opposition by making sure human rights activists don't turn up dead in the morning news."

A weary sigh came over the line. *"Ken, I know you don't want to hear this, but innocent people are going to get caught in the cross fire. No black market on earth right now is more profitable than baby labs, and the syndicates that run them are ruthless. They've killed journalists, police, politicians, civilians. Their bad press will far exceed ours. Mark my words: the public will stay the course with us, even if, like this morning, we have some bad news days."*

Durand drummed his fingers on a nearby railing. "It's more than a bad news day to me."

"Ken. You didn't kill Ms. Cherian."

Durand stared at nothing. "I wrote the algorithms that found that lab. She is dead because—"

"A cop with bad aim killed Ms. Cherian. She was just at the wrong place at the wrong time."

Durand paced in silence.

"We save lives every day by shutting down these labs. You know it's true."

Durand remained silent.

"Hang in there, buddy. Listen, I'll see you at the eight o'clock. Okay?"

"Right."

"Haeng-syo."

Durand closed the line.

The building's AI asked, *"Shall I summon an elevator, Mr. Durand?"*

Durand nodded, mopping sweat from his face with his Annapolis T-shirt. He resisted the innate human urge to thank the digital assistant and walked toward the elevator bank.

Chapter 3

Durand padded down a corridor lined with culture-grown hardwoods and printed metals. The decor had an elegant, Scandinavian simplicity. The door to his flat recognized him and *clicked* unlocked as he reached it.

He pushed inside and gave a tight smile. "Morning."

His wife, Miyuki Uchida, sat at her desk with a cup of tea, engaged in an AR video conference with people invisible to Durand. Actual physical, framed photos of family, friends, and colleagues, along with mementos from years of development work in Africa, lined the shelves behind her. Her long black hair shimmered in the morning light as she turned a smile toward him, then blinded the line. "Hey, you."

He kissed her on the cheek. "You're up early."

"My Accra team ran into permit problems. Now they're talking in circles."

"Can I make you something?" Durand went into the kitchen.

"Thanks. I already ate. There's a mangosteen in there for you."

Durand filled a bottle of chilled water from the fridge door. In a few moments his wife followed him into the kitchen.

"Birthday girl up yet?" Durand grabbed a white tropical fruit from the fridge.

"Pretending to sleep—which reminds me: don't forget to come home with her gift tonight."

"Why wasn't it delivered here?"

"She's scanning deliveries."

"Ah."

"Something's bothering you. I can tell."

Durand took a bite of the mangosteen. After a moment he shrugged. "Just work stuff."

She regarded him.

He squirmed under her gaze.

"I haven't seen that look in two years."

Durand blinked. "My analysis got a civilian killed. Last night. A young woman. Human rights activist."

She put a hand on his shoulder. "Oh, Ken. I'm sorry." She hesitated. "Although I'm guessing it's not as simple as that."

"I can't get into the details."

"I understand." She hugged him. "I'm so sorry."

"This is why I got out, Mi."

"I know, but this isn't the same thing, Ken."

"It's happening all over again."

"It isn't the same." She let go and looked at him. "No one's launching air strikes based on your analysis."

He said nothing.

She took his hand. "You know how guilty living in the Bubble makes me feel. There's so much trouble in the world. We promised each other that we would only do this if what we're doing here makes the world a better place for her generation." She pointed at the refrigerator.

Durand turned to see a printed photo pinned to the fridge of their daughter's robotics team competing at a local maker fair. Smiling young hopeful faces.

"I know you well enough to know that's what you're trying to do."

He stared at the photo and nodded reluctantly. Then he noticed one of his daughter's plesiosaur polygon models pinned up nearby. He tapped the teacher's gold star affixed to it and nodded to his wife appreciatively. "She's getting good."

"Of course. She takes after me."

He laughed in spite of himself. "I'm gonna grab a shower."

• • •

While Durand ran an electric razor over his face, the family cat sat on the bathroom counter, watching him. Genetically modified, the breed was known as a "toyger" because it perfectly resembled a miniature tiger. The cat's gaze unnerved him—as though a full-grown tiger watched from the far bank of some watering hole instead of the far side of the bathroom sink.

"Nelson, do you mind?"

The toyger answered with a rumbling meow.

His daughter's pet. For some reason it focused most of its attention on Durand. He wasn't thrilled with the idea of bespoke animals. However, neotenic pets—the cuter and more juvenile, the better—were all the rage these days. And golden retrievers weren't an option in HDB flats.

After shaving, Durand got dressed, knotted his tie, pulled on his suit jacket, and gathered his devices before heading down the hall. He knocked before poking his head into his daughter's room, Nelson still close on his heels.

His daughter's room was decorated with solar system mobiles, deep field survey posters, and 3D-printed robot dinosaurs she'd created. He gazed down on her sleeping form.

She looked peaceful, a plush dinosaur toy pressed against her cheek.

He whispered, "You're such a faker."

Mia opened her eyes and giggled. "You woke me up."

"Really." He sat on the edge of her bed. "If you were asleep, then what's this . . . ?" He reached under her pillow and produced a glim. Already powered up, the small dome-shaped device instantly located his eyes and projected a video game screen onto his retinas. A virtual aquarium suddenly floated in midair before him—alive with alien swimming creatures and fictional plant life.

"Remember that talk we had about the importance of sleep?"

She whined, "I *did* sleep."

"So if I check the log on this device, I'm not going to see you were up all night?"

"It's *gamework*. And it's due today."

"Gamework."

"Yes. But I couldn't solve it."

Durand examined the screen and the completion percentage in the lower-right corner . . . slowly decrementing: 72 percent . . . then 71. "Well, if I can make some suggestions. Your ecosystem is out of balance—that's why it's decaying."

She propped herself up on her elbows.

He pointed. "You need more diversity to close your life cycle."

"How do I do that?"

"Well, see how energy is draining with each generation? Who's cleaning the ocean floor and recirculating nutrients up the food chain?"

She frowned at the image, which the glim was now projecting into both of their eyes.

"You created big creatures—which is fun. But notice how they're dying off? Instead make tiny, simple creatures, and they'll evolve from there. Balanced ecosystems grow from the bottom up over time, not from the top down all at once. We don't *design* complex systems; we evolve them. It's what Nature does. And Nature is the best teacher."

She reached out to the virtual aquarium and started creating tiny organisms from building blocks on the ocean floor with practiced flicks of her hand—quickly getting engrossed in the simulation.

The percentage jumped to 83. Then to 84. Then 85.

"There you go." He swept her hair aside and kissed her on the forehead. "You're welcome."

She spoke without looking up from the screen. "Adele was wrong. I told her she was wrong."

"It's not Adele's job to do *your* thinking." He got up.

Mia looked up at him. "Daddy?"

"Yes?"

"Is it wrong to edit babies?"

Durand paused for a moment but then sat back down on the edge of her bed. "What makes you ask *that*?"

"Because I was edited. Does that make me a bad person?" Mia kept working on the simulation.

Durand sat in shocked silence for several moments. "Who says you were edited?"

"You did." She turned to him. "I heard you talking to Jiichan when he and Obaasan came to visit."

Durand closed his eyes in frustration at his own stupidity. "Well, first: you weren't meant to hear that."

"So it *is* wrong?"

"No. Well, *babies* don't get edited; *embryos* get edited—when they're just a single fertilized cell. And it's rare."

She looked up at him. "Adele's mom says babies—I mean, embryos—should never be edited."

"Editing isn't necessarily wrong, and it's nothing to be ashamed of."

"But you and Sergeant Yi arrest people for editing embryos."

He leaned down to press his forehead against hers. "No, hon. Daddy doesn't *arrest* anyone. All I do is help the police find people who break the law."

"But editing is against the law."

"Not all edits—just those that aren't safe."

"Was mine safe?"

"Yes."

"What kind of edit was it?"

"It was to cure a disorder—one that's hard to pronounce, but it's called Leber congenital amaurosis. It would have caused your eyes not to develop, so you'd be blind. The doctors made a tiny edit to your SPATA7 gene and fixed it so you could grow up and see the world."

"So it cured me."

He nodded. "That's right. There's nothing wrong with curing an illness. I'm sure Adele's mom takes medicine when she's sick. People correct bad eyesight and cure diseases. Right?"

She nodded.

"Well, that's what your mom and I did because we love you very much."

"Then why are people on the feeds so upset?"

"They're not upset at you, honey."

"What are they mad at?"

He paused again. "Like I said: it's complicated. That's why we wanted to wait until you were older to talk about this." Realizing she wasn't satisfied with this, he added, "Some people want to edit embryos even when they're not sick."

"Why?"

"Because they want to make their kids taller or stronger or smarter than other kids."

"But some kids *are* stronger and taller and smarter."

"Yes, but Nature does that."

"But Nature also makes kids sick—like I was."

Durand paused. "That's true." He laughed and thought harder. "But we don't fully understand how all our genes work together. They took millions of years to evolve, and any changes we make are passed down to all future generations. So the results could change our whole species in ways we didn't intend . . ." A thought occurred to him. "Like in your gamework." He gestured to the glim-cast image. "Do you see how traits in your creatures are passed down to following generations?"

She nodded.

"Well, that's how genetics works in the real world. When you took a shortcut and designed your creatures the way you wanted, they didn't fit the environment, did they?"

She shook her head.

"And even though they looked cool, they soon got sick, and their offspring even sicker—and soon your whole ecosystem got sick. The same is true in the real world. If we make edits that don't fit the environment— even though we think they're cool—then bad things could happen to future generations that we didn't expect. And we don't want that. That's why we only let sick people correct genetic errors—changes that will make them the way humans evolved to be. Any other edits are against the law. And those are the edits your daddy, Sergeant Yi, and Inspector Belanger try to stop—because we want to keep everyone safe."

She looked up at him.

He brushed her hair away from her eyes. "Someday I'm sure you'll know a lot more than I do about all this."

She laughed. "I don't think so. You know a lot."

"You'd be surprised." He glanced up at the time. "Now, if I'm gonna get to work on time, I've got to go." He kissed her on the forehead and confiscated the glim. "Happy birthday, kiddo. And don't fall asleep at school."

He went to the door. "I'll see you tonight."

She waved. "Bye, Daddy."

"Bye-bye, sweetheart." Durand closed the door and turned to see his wife standing in the hall.

She smiled as she approached him. Then she put her arms around his neck. "The birds and the bees are so twentieth century."

"The birds and the bees I *can* explain. Or at least I think I can. What do the birds do again?"

She kissed him. "You did great. It almost makes me forget how badly you screwed up."

He winced. "I know. She must have been eavesdropping with one of her drones. You know how she gets when there's company."

"Thankfully, it worked out." Miyuki held out her hand.

Durand placed the glim into her outstretched palm.

"See you tonight." She kissed him. "Don't forget her gift."

"I won't. I won't."

Chapter 4

nterpol's Global Complex for Innovation, or GCI, resembled a fortified modern art museum. Originally built in the teens of the twenty-first century, it had been expanded and hardened against attack over the years. It now covered several acres of prime real estate in Singapore's diplomatic quarter across Napier Road from the US embassy.

As he approached the entrance, Kenneth Durand nodded to armed guards watching from beyond transparent aluminum blast shields marked with Interpol's sword-and-globe logo. The entrance split into a dozen sealed chutes, only one of which opened to admit Durand. The chute doors operated on a randomized algorithm—with each visitor following a separate, illuminated path. The entire entry system was designed to identify and categorize people into risk tranches—moving them through without stopping and quickly isolating suspected threats. This way no one queued up, which itself would have presented a target to terrorists.

And the GCI was definitely a target.

Organized into financial, cyber, genetic, and counterterrorism divisions, Interpol's GCI employed advanced technologies in the fight against transnational crime—though, contrary to popular perception, Interpol agents themselves had no police powers (at least outside their home countries). Likewise, Interpol itself had only two facilities worldwide—this GCI complex and a headquarters in Lyon, France.

Instead, 190 national police organizations around the world maintained their own Interpol National Central Bureaus, assigning officers to liaise with Interpol's network, receiving and issuing a kaleidoscope of colored Notices—Red, Orange, Yellow, Blue, Green, Purple, Black— advising other nations on the activities of global criminals and the increasingly borderless world of crime. Whether other nations followed up on those Notices depended on local politics and priorities. But if national police organizations wanted cooperation from other national police around the world, ignoring Interpol Notices wasn't the way to get it. This quid pro quo arrangement had worked with varying levels of success over the decades.

Member nations occasionally assigned—or *seconded*—investigators directly to Interpol headquarters, usually to learn or teach about new types of crime. And when it came to catching the next generation of high-tech criminals, Interpol was prepared to recruit from more than just the ranks of police.

Kenneth Durand was fortunate to be one of those recruits. And it couldn't have come at a more propitious time for him, personally.

He cleared two more security checkpoints before arriving on the third floor and passing through another transparent aluminum blast wall emblazoned with the seal of the Genetic Crime Division—Interpol's standard logo with the addition of a twining double helix of DNA around the sword, itself an alarming mutation to Asclepius's staff.

Durand entered the busy offices, nodding at a passing lab techni- cian. The floor plan was sleek, modern—but crowded with makeshift workstations. Proprietary DNA theft, custom viruses, and baby labs were fast becoming the world's most profitable criminal enterprises. That meant the Genetic Crime Division was growing fast, too.

Durand entered the small, windowless office he shared with Detec- tive Sergeant Michael Yi Ji-chang. "Morning, Mike."

"Hey." Yi stared at an AR screen (or screens) only he could see. Yi was an athletic, handsome man. He'd been seconded to Interpol from the Korean National Police Agency in Seoul, which had been in turmoil ever since the reunification. He was here to share his expertise in embryo clinic cartels—and it was Yi who'd referred Durand to Interpol.

"Something up?" Durand removed his suit jacket.

"Oh, sorry. No. Just reading a note from my new cousin."

"New? They found another one?"

"Yeah. Ministry of Health ran his DNA. Confirmed he's related."

"Congratulations. You're getting quite an extended family."

"Wants to come live with me."

"Shit."

"Blew through his reuni check. No marketable job skills. Fan-fucking-tastic." Yi dismissed the virtual screen that was distracting him. "You look better than you sounded on the phone."

Durand hung his suit jacket behind the door. "Haven't changed my mind, though."

"Let's schedule an argument. Right now we've got our eight o'clock." Yi got up and grabbed his own suit jacket from the back of his chair, then headed out through the cubicles.

"Oh, right." Durand grabbed his coat again and caught up. "The calendar just said 'external briefing.' What's this about—the Mumbai raid?"

Yi shook his head. "Two hundred and sixty-three embryo mills shut down on three continents last month, and you think top brass is upset about Mumbai?"

"I'm telling you, it matters."

Durand's division lead, Detective Inspector Claire Belanger, stood at the head of the briefing room. She was a slim, elegant woman in her early fifties, with a sweep of gray hair and piercing blue eyes. She wore a tailored pantsuit and no jewelry save for a platinum wedding band. Durand knew it had been placed there by her late husband—before the bioweapon attack in Paris, an attack that not only killed Belanger's husband but also sterilized thousands of Parisians, Belanger among them. Calm but intense, originally a biochemist, she had joined the Police Nationale in France and was later seconded to Interpol—where she now led the war against genetic crime. Life had delivered her here. Durand could think of no one more capable.

Belanger spoke English with a slight French accent. "Good morning. I realize this briefing was called with little notice, but it will cover new intelligence critical to our mission."

Belanger studied the faces of the two dozen members in her section. Satisfied she had their attention, Belanger continued. "We are joined today by Detective Inspector Aiyana Marcotte, head of Interpol's Human Trafficking Task Force. She will bring you up to speed. Inspector Marcotte comes to Interpol from the US Federal Bureau of Investigation. She is an experienced field agent who, as you'll soon learn, has unique expertise in global human trafficking networks. I expect your full attention to all she has to say—because it will change what we do." Belanger nodded to someone in the audience. "Inspector Marcotte."

"Thank you, Inspector Belanger." A statuesque African woman in her early thirties stood, her skin dark black, hair cropped short. She had a strong jawline and slender neck. Marcotte wore a dark blue business suit. Interpol identification hung around her neck on a lanyard, though Durand knew this was primarily for the convenience of staffers—the GCI's security systems recognized all people within its walls.

Belanger took a seat in the first row as Marcotte moved to the head of the room to stand before Interpol's official seal. Marcotte gazed out at the expert agents and analysts.

"In 2039, sixty million people attempted migrations northward and southward, away from regions stressed by drought, groundwater depletion, rising seas, corruption, war, or economic despair. By 2043, that number had swelled to seventy million. This year, the number is expected to increase yet again.

"Trafficking human beings involves more than just transporting migrants over borders. When people leave behind everything they own and everything they know—language, culture, family—they become vulnerable to exploitation. And exploitation is primarily what human trafficking gangs engage in."

Marcotte gestured and a virtual map of the world's continents appeared in midair. Opaque and vibrant, the image was beamed directly into the retinas of her audience by the room's LFP—or light field projection—system. It closely tracked the eye movement of every person in the room, and was capable of beaming to a full audience.

Marcotte gestured to the map of the world. Moving arrows illustrated paths of human migration away from equatorial climes.

"You may be familiar with these migration routes. Prostitution, manual labor—or worse—awaits the unlucky at the end of these journeys. Stripped of their few possessions, many will have accrued massive 'debts' to the traffickers who smuggle them—debts that must be repaid wherever they arrive."

Marcotte waved and the map was replaced by a gallery of life-sized and extraordinarily lifelike 3D scenes of refugees from all around the world—Caucasians, Africans, Latinos, Arabs, Central and Southeast Asians—men, women, children. These life-sized, realistic forms brought the full emotional impact of poverty to the audience in a way mere photos could not. The victims, frozen in time, had seemingly been brought into the room, new scenes fading in as old ones faded out. A never-ending procession of hardship.

Marcotte walked among the virtual migrants and stood. She gazed out at her audience.

"I, too, was trafficked as a child. In Sudan, my mother sold me into slavery at the age of six—so that my brothers could attend school. I was sold to a wealthy family, consular officials, who later brought me with them to the United States as a domestic. And it was in their home in a gated suburb of Los Angeles that I worked seven days a week and was chained to a bed each night. It was only when neighbors became suspicious that the police were called and I was freed. The arresting female officer later adopted me. Raised me as her own. And it is her name that I took."

She met the eyes of her audience. "Slavery is not an abstraction to me. I have experienced it. I have firsthand knowledge of the despair it brings, and that it is not in our past. In fact, there are more slaves in existence now than at any point in human history. The question is: What are we going to do about it?"

The entire room sat in stunned silence.

"I've come to seek the assistance of the Genetic Crime Division. Your group is one of the few success stories in the fight against high-tech transnational crime. All of Interpol has much to learn from you."

She studied the faces in the room. "And today I'm going to show you evidence that the worlds of human trafficking and genetic crime are converging."

A brief susurration spread through her audience.

She motioned and the images of refugees dissolved, soon replaced by a dozen full-body, hyperrealistic 3D booking scans of heavily tattooed criminals slowly rotating as if on a vertical rotisserie. Each virtual prisoner held a plaque displaying their name and booking number. The group was ethnically diverse—Caucasians, Africans, Asians, Latinos—hard-eyed men, plus a couple of women.

"These are captured leaders of human trafficking gangs that my task force disrupted in the past year." She pointed. "Asia; Africa; Russia; Europe; North, South, and Central America. These gangs all have one thing in common: they've been harvesting genetic material from the refugees they traffic—and selling that data to a single genediting cartel, a group known as the Huli jing. Does that name mean anything here in the GCD?"

Durand nodded with others around him. "We're familiar with the name, Inspector. They're a black market, on-demand cloud computing service. Used by embryo mills for genetic modeling."

Yi added, "Their ties to human trafficking is news to us. You say they pay for DNA samples?"

Marcotte nodded. "Digitized samples. The per-head bounty varies by country. We first learned of it from informants who were being required to extract DNA samples from refugees—saliva swabs mostly. Petabytes of genetic information were being sent from four continents to the Huli jing on a daily basis in exchange for cryptocurrency payments."

Durand took notes on a virtual surface. "It sounds like they're building a global genetic database."

Marcotte nodded. "That's precisely what the Huli jing is doing, Mr. Durand. In fact, we have evidence they were involved in the recent compromise of the Chinese National Genetic Registry—the largest digital storehouse of human genetic information in the world."

More murmurs spread through the audience.

Marcotte paced. "The Huli jing is well funded, disciplined, and extremely low-profile—with a data-gathering operation that gives them globe-spanning influence over both illicit editing labs and human trafficking rings. So far they've fallen between the cracks because they don't directly participate in either activity. But it's time we realized how pivotal they are to both and put our heads together to deal with them. So who are the Huli jing?"

Her entire audience was tapping notes into virtual devices now.

"The name *Huli jing* refers to a mythological nine-tailed fox spirit from Chinese lore, an entity able to assume any form—able to perpetrate mischief while remaining undetected." With a gesture, an inset image of a stylized fox appeared:

"The fox spirit has long been a popular tattoo throughout Asia and the West. But don't look for it among the Huli jing; unlike most gangs they themselves bear no distinguishing marks. No tattoos or brands. Like the mythological fox spirit, they prefer to remain hidden. How do we know?"

She waved her hand and the nine-tailed fox image faded away—replaced by 3D morgue scans of a dozen dead men of many different races—their faces in various stages of decomposition. Nude, the bodies had not one tattoo among them. "Because until recently these men were members of the Huli jing's inner circle—referred to as the Nine Tails—and they bore no gang symbols whatsoever."

Yi grunted. "They're dead."

"Good eye, Sergeant. Yes, they are dead."

And then another set of equally dead faces appeared. And then another.

"And so are these. And these. This last batch from just a month ago. None of the Nine Tails live long. Many were already dead before they'd been identified by our informants. We only discovered their identities later."

Durand frowned in confusion. "Murdered by rival gangs?"

"No. Poisoned by the leader of the Huli jing—Marcus Demang Wyckes. Our best guess is that he *murders* his inner circle on a regular basis."

Looks of confusion spread throughout the audience.

Yi frowned. "Then who on earth would want to become one of the Nine Tails?"

"An excellent question."

Marcotte pointed at the rogues gallery. "These men were all refugees. Perhaps they admired Wyckes—because, like them, Wyckes grew up in refugee camps. And yet he rose to become a major arms smuggler to a dozen insurgencies and terrorist groups. Wyckes gave these men a life of unimagined luxury and power for a brief time. Let them send significant sums of money to their extended families back home. And when they were no longer useful, he eliminated them. Apparently there is no shortage of desperate people willing to make that deal. Only one man always survives among the leadership of the Huli jing—and that's Marcus Wyckes."

Durand watched the procession of morgue scans continue. Each dead face both a victim and a willing participant. "I don't see how men with little education or training could manage—"

"Neither do we, Mr. Durand. That's what I'm hoping your group will help us explain. The Huli jing is a highly technical criminal organization with complex logistical needs, and yet somehow it continues to operate even though its leadership is constantly dying off. It's like no other cartel we've seen. There's no way to place high-level informants. Or to make arrests. Anyone who knows anything important soon dies. All except Wyckes."

Marcotte dismissed the dead men with a wave of her hand. "And as ruthless as Wyckes is with his own people—he is even more terrible to his enemies . . ."

She gestured, and several gruesome, hyperrealistic crime-scene scans appeared onstage—as real as if they were in the room. Each depicted victims dead of some hemorrhagic agent, blood streaming from eyes, nose, mouth. The victims clearly died screaming. "The preferred weapon of the Huli jing is poison—specifically custom-designed synbio-toxins that are difficult to detect and which maximize the victim's agony."

The audience reacted with muted disgust.

Molecular diagrams appeared alongside each image. "We suspect these biotoxins are developed in Huli jing labs—possibly customized to exploit genetic weaknesses of individual targets, meaning doses can be microscopic. Government officials, police, journalists are all fair game—anyone who tries to interfere with the Huli jing's business, which is developing and selling new genetic edits."

The entire room was furiously tapping notes.

"They have, in effect, created a franchise operation—one where they do not directly operate genetic labs, but provide the logistical, research, and even marketing support to gangs that do. Huli jing partner labs benefit from access to the most sophisticated technology. They've even branded their select franchisees with a premium label." Marcotte waved her hand and a three-sided knot replaced the crime-scene images:

It rotated, showing the depth of the knot in three-dimensional space. "Do any of you recognize this symbol?"

Durand, Yi, and most people in the division nodded. "Yes. That's the logo for Trefoil Labs."

Marcotte walked around the image. "Trefoil *is* the public face of the Huli jing."

Durand captured the logo and pasted it into his notes. "That's a very useful piece of intelligence, Inspector."

Marcotte nodded. "Their impressive edit library is expanding because they use massive photonic computing clusters to comb through oceans of global genetic data, discovering novel, commercially valuable mutations."

Durand: "They're expanding the edits available to parents."

"Correct—meaning your challenge here at the GCD is going to grow."

Another murmur swept through the crowd.

"More worrisome, the Huli jing is performing unethical research to confirm the viability of the edits their computer models predict . . ." With a wave of her hand, grainy two-dimensional photos appeared, depicting hideously deformed infants. Horrifying mutations.

The audience reacted with gasps.

"These images were taken by hidden camera. This is what Marcus Wyckes is capable of. The Huli jing is mapping not just the human genome, but epigenetics—gene expression—turning genes on and off. And they're doing it with no regard for human suffering. They've also been paying human traffickers to steal the eggs of young women unfortunate enough to fall under their control. To provide raw material for their research."

Durand noticed smoldering rage in Belanger's eyes as she looked up at the images.

"They're developing new edits and searching for commercially valuable mutations present in the population at large. And as you know, mutation laundering can revise the provenance of genetic IP—potentially turning single mutations into multibillion-dollar commercial products. Providing a strong economic incentive for governments to turn a blind eye to their activity."

Durand felt a burden lift from him as he exchanged looks with Yi. The sergeant had been right after all—their work was indeed critically important. More important than he'd ever guessed. He felt a renewed sense of purpose.

Marcotte swept the images all away. "One individual lies at the center of all of this: Marcus Demang Wyckes. He is the single unchanging fact of the Huli jing—its founder and its reclusive leader. If we can locate him, I think we can break their organization—and remove its support of both illicit baby labs and human trafficking cartels."

Marcotte studied the faces in the room. "Here is the last known photograph of Marcus Wyckes . . ." Marcotte waved her hand and a two-dimensional, old-time police booking photo appeared. It showed a dark-haired, burly Eurasian teenager with tan skin. Still young, Wyckes was nonetheless physically intimidating, with broad shoulders, a square jaw, and menacing eyes. "This is from a 2029 arrest in Vietnam on weapon smuggling charges."

Yi piped in, "That picture is fifteen years old."

"Which is why DNA samples taken from Vietnamese and Australian authorities were so useful. We were able to extract his complete genetic sequence and model his physical appearance at his current age of thirty-eight. We've predicted his height within five centimeters precision, his BMI within eight kilograms of precision, his eye color, skin color, and his facial structure." She looked out at her audience. "This is Marcus Wyckes now."

A virtual, photographically real computer model of Marcus Wyckes appeared bald-headed and nude, rotating before them, hands held at his side—a modesty filter blurring out his genitals. His facial expression neutral. One could clearly see the Malay-Australian ethnic mix with his tan skin. He looked physically powerful. Average height, but muscular, with a thick neck and slim waist even in his late thirties. Wyckes's physical stats appeared in text alongside—height, weight, age, eye color, and more.

"Yesterday my group issued a Red Notice for Wyckes's capture in every Interpol member country. I'm hoping I can count on your assistance in that effort."

A strong chorus of assent spread throughout the room.

Belanger stood. "Inspector, I speak for everyone here when I say we will do all within our power to assist you."

"Thank you, Inspector Belanger." She turned to the other agents and analysts. "I thank you for your time."

Belanger turned to her division staff. "You will find the dossier for Marcus Wyckes, the Huli jing, and all relevant intelligence relating to their activities on the GCD Commons. Within the next forty-eight hours I expect to see action plans from group leaders on how to pursue the Huli jing—with an eye in particular on locating Marcus Wyckes. That is all."

As the briefing broke up, Marcotte approached Durand and Yi, extending her hand to Durand. "Mr. Durand."

Surprised, Durand met her eyes and shook firmly. "Great detective work, Inspector Marcotte. I hope you know you can count on us."

Marcotte nodded. "I have it on good authority that your data mining is the root of the GCD's success against embryo labs."

Durand cast a glance at Belanger, who just now joined them.

Belanger nodded the okay to Durand.

He turned back to Marcotte. "I prefer the term *geospatial analysis*."

"Call it what you like, it means culling through oceans of data—not unlike the Huli jing."

"I think it's very different. My work doesn't involve genetic data at all. Just data on human activity."

"Where do you get it?"

"We purchase it just like any marketing company—but instead of targeting customers, we're looking for criminal enterprises."

Marcotte studied Durand for a moment. "I was told that early in your career you helped locate serial killers by modeling honey bees."

Durand was surprised she knew of his master's thesis. Apparently Marcotte had done her homework. "I just found a useful behavior pattern shared by both."

"And what behavior do honey bees and serial killers have in common?"

"Bee brains are fairly simple, so it's easier to model how bees are recruited to flowers than it is to understand how serial killers are drawn toward victims. However, both follow certain elemental behaviors. Bees, for example, maintain a buffer zone around their hive—a zone where they do not forage—in order to avoid bringing unwanted attention to the location of their home. Likewise, the data indicates most serial killers kill in the region of their home, but not in the immediate vicinity of it, where they're more likely to run into someone who recognizes them. Therefore, mapping the geographic spread of a killer's victims helps to further pinpoint the home base of a killer—narrowing the search area with every murder. The mathematical model closely correlates with bee-foraging algorithms."

"Interesting. Your CV says you spent eight years with US Naval Intelligence—hunting down gene-drive bioweapons. Why'd you leave?"

Durand felt an emotional scar itch somewhere deep. "I can't discuss that."

Yi interjected, "Ken did his share, Inspector."

Marcotte relented. "Of course. In any event, it's Interpol's gain. Mr. Durand, your group has achieved more against the Huli jing in the past six months than the rest of Interpol combined. You've seriously hampered their lab network."

Durand nodded. "Good."

"Your success is one reason I've come. I'd like you to focus your data-mining skills on the effort to locate Marcus Wyckes."

Durand exchanged looks with Yi, then Belanger. Then he looked back to Marcotte. "We find criminal activity, not individuals."

"My task force wants to stop human trafficking, and you want to stop genetic crime. The Huli jing are now at the center of both. And Marcus Wyckes is its driving force. Without him, we're confident his group will splinter."

There was silence for a few moments.

"Without question we'll assist you any way we can, Inspector. But regardless of what you've heard, geospatial analysis is not suited to locating specific individuals. I learned that the hard way. What it is useful for is identifying a pattern consistent with certain activities."

"Wyckes must have a pattern."

"Which we can't possibly know." Durand felt old fears awakening. "Individuals are far too variable. Too specific. You will get false positives. Innocent people will die."

Yi touched Durand's shoulder. "Ken."

Durand took a moment. "My algorithms have located hundreds of illegal CRISPR labs in dozens of countries—but we weren't looking for individuals. We were looking for a pattern of illicit commercial activity—a specific location that attracted would-be or existing parents who matched a consistent profile. Parents who had recently deviated from their established behavior patterns. Spent money on fertility treatments. Changed their usual travel and social patterns—especially after meeting with friends who'd recently done the same. We've issued Orange Notices to police agencies based on that analysis, but not Red Notices calling for individual arrests. That lies beyond the data."

"There must be some way to narrow down the search area for Wyckes or for his center of operations, like you did with your serial killer algorithms."

Durand was already shaking his head. "Again, organizations don't behave like individuals, and in any event, I doubt that Wyckes is taking part directly in crimes. Those would most likely be these Nine Tails you showed us."

"Then the activities of the Huli jing create a pattern."

"Yes, and if the Huli jing are selling new edits to illicit genetic editing labs on several continents, then our efforts will impact their business. However, locating Marcus Wyckes *cannot* be part of our mission—not directly." Durand looked up to realize he was raising his voice. "I'm sorry, Inspector. Perhaps in one of these lab raids we'll get lucky, and intel on Wyckes's whereabouts will be found."

Yi added, "You must understand, Inspector, Ken's analysis has been forced to fit a pressing need before. Didn't turn out so well."

Marcotte relented. "I understand."

Belanger stepped in. "Inspector Marcotte, what you've shown us today makes the Huli jing our most pressing priority."

Marcotte nodded. "Sorry if I pressed you, Mr. Durand. I'd heard that you have a knack for locating things hiding in the data. But I also respect that you know the limits of your tools." She reached into her coat pocket. "If by chance anything does occur to you—a moment of inspiration perhaps—don't hesitate to contact me directly." She handed Durand an actual physical business card.

Puzzled, Durand took it and examined the inscrutable email address on it.

"I gather you don't get handed a lot of business cards."

He laughed. "No. It's kind of quaint. So you still use email?"

"It's helpful for informants. Some of the people who need to reach me are very poor and don't trust social media platforms."

Durand blinked at the card, and his LFP glasses scraped the data into his contacts.

Before she turned to go, Marcotte touched Durand's elbow. "If you don't mind my asking, how did a guy who can't locate individual criminals wind up finding so many of them?"

Durand thought for a moment. "No offense, but I think the mistake of traditional law enforcement technique is its focus on individuals. Here, we try to limit the damage and spread of *criminal activity*—and that's what drives arrests at the local level. Individual criminals are in some ways beneath our notice here. What we defeat are rising trends. That's why guys like Wyckes never see us coming—because, in many ways, not even we realize we're looking for them."

Marcotte stared. "I see. Well, I look forward to working with you in the future, Mr. Durand."

"Likewise, Inspector."

Chapter 5

Early evening, and Durand sat in the conditioned air of a private, autonomous comcar as it merged into the close coordination of rush hour. His daughter's wrapped birthday gift sat on the seat beside him. He leaned back and felt the stress of the day leave him.

In the distance he could see the glowing logos of synbio firms on the Singapore skyline. Licensed AR video ads played across the surfaces of several skyscrapers—although they were really only being beamed into Durand's retinas by his own LFP glasses. The contract for his LFP glasses required exposure to specific layers of public advertising. At least he'd opted out of the low-end ads, but opting out of all AR advertising was prohibitively expensive.

Just the same, Durand frowned at the shoddy data management employed by advertisers. He was clearly not in the target demographic for an ad gliding across neighboring buildings, alive with images of Jedis, Starfleet officers, and steampunk characters: *"Singapore's premier Star Wars*™, *Star Trek*™, *and steampunk cosliving communities . . ."*

Cosseted young professionals at the big synbio firms were a more likely demo for their product—single people with a couple million to blow on living in a theme park.

But by then the ad had shifted to CRISPR Critters. Gigantic, adorable neotenic cats cavorted from building to building, pursuing a virtual ball of yarn.

Durand decided to close his eyes.

He knew it was extravagant to have his own private comcar, but it was one of the perks of the job. And in fact, he treasured this time each day. He had never really had time alone growing up. Not enough space for that. No privacy at the Naval Academy, either, and certainly not in the service.

Durand considered turning on some music when he heard the car's familiar voice.

"Rerouting . . . Revised travel time one hour and six minutes."

Durand sat up. His commute had suddenly tripled in length. The comcar was stopped at a traffic light. Hundreds of people passed on the crosswalk in front of it. He turned around to look through the rear windshield at smaller, older building facades. The towering buildings of the Central Business District stood behind him—which meant he wasn't heading toward the BKE anymore. The car was taking a new route.

"Shit."

Traffic must be backed up somewhere. In his LFP glasses he brought up the car's virtual map and expanded it. The new route brought him around a line of red traffic warnings on the expressway.

"Damnit . . ." Durand tapped his LFP glasses to phone home.

In a moment Miyuki's voice came on the line. *"Hi, hon."*

"Hi, Mi."

"I'm scrambling to get ready. Please tell me you remembered the gift."

"Yes, got it right here." He put a hand on the package. "Just wanted to let you know the comcar is routing around traffic. If it keeps going this way I'm going to be late."

"What's your ETA?"

Durand winced. "Over an hour, but I'm working on it. Just wanted to give you a heads-up."

"Okay. Do what you can. Love you."

"Love you, too."

He clicked off and watched in surprise as the comcar signaled and pulled slowly over to the left curb. The car's interior lights illuminated as if he'd opened the door.

The car's AI voice said, *"This vehicle is experiencing technical difficulties. Please exit."*

He shouted at the ceiling liner. "Oh, come on!"

"Please exit the vehicle. This vehicle is now out of service."

"Goddamnit . . ." Durand grabbed Mia's gift and got out. He glanced around to get his bearings. He was clearly in an older part of the city. He instantiated the virtual map again with his LFP glasses and studied it as it floated before him.

He then launched his car-hailing app and noticed that it had terminated his ride due to an unspecified vehicle malfunction. Oddly, the app had not summoned a replacement car. He clicked through and was rewarded with an estimated pickup time of forty-five minutes from now.

"No, no, no." The car service had just dumped him here, far off the main expressways. In the middle of rush hour he knew damn well the algorithms were going to triage him as the odd man out. There was no efficient way to collect him where he was.

"Not today. Goddamnit." He checked the time. Guests were showing up in an hour and a half.

Commuters passed him on foot. They, too, were focused on or talking to their own devices.

Just then the supposedly out-of-service comcar he'd exited closed its doors and drove away—merging into the traffic.

"Are you shitting me?" Durand ran alongside the car on the sidewalk, pushing through the foot traffic. "Excuse me. Pardon me."

But the car didn't stop. He glanced at the ride-hailing app again, but no, he'd definitely lost his link to the vehicle. It drove off with an out-of-service AR sign rotating above it.

Durand sighed in frustration as other commuters continued to swarm past him. In a moment it occurred to him that they all seemed to be walking with purpose. He opened the map again and zoomed in to his current location. He was close to the new Tekka wet market—and an MRT station. If he couldn't get a car, he could take the MRT. He examined the street detail.

There. MRT station two blocks away. Durand oriented himself and now realized why the passersby were turning down a narrow pedestrian lane between historic brick buildings of the Little India district. It was the shortest path to the train station.

The north-south line stopped just a few blocks from his building. This was salvageable.

He tapped his LFP glasses to make a call as he fell in line with the rest of the foot traffic.

Miyuki answered. *"How's it looking?"*

He laughed. "You're not gonna believe this. My comcar crapped out."

"You're kidding."

"Stranded me in Little India before it shut down, and it'll take forty-five minutes for another car to pick me up."

"That's ridiculous."

"Don't worry. There's an MRT station nearby. I can hop a train. This might turn out better actually. I might not even be late."

"Well, make sure they give you a credit."

"I have to pay attention to where I'm going, though. So I'm going to hang up. See you soon, hon."

"Bye."

He clicked off and followed other commuters down a narrow lane between old brick buildings. This MRT crowd skewed young—twenties and early thirties. Lots of expats. Well dressed and all talking to people who weren't there. Snatches of conversation floated past him in Hokkien, Mandarin, Malay, Tamil, English, Russian, Swahili, German, Korean—and more he didn't recognize. They'd no doubt come to Singapore to make their killing. To work threads in a blockchain corporation or license their own cellular machinery. XNA programmers. Genetic engineers. Entrepreneurs. And they all had to have impressive CVs to get a work visa in the city.

Looking up, Durand noticed the old Indian and Hokkien storefronts around them. He wondered how these shops and tiny exporters were hanging on. Singapore was not a town paralyzed by nostalgia. Durand had never seen poorly designed public spaces in the city, and that's what this historic district was. He got jostled and held tightly on to Mia's gift as the crowd grew dense. It surged toward the MRT station entrance. Streams of commuters pushed and shoved.

Carried along with the crowd, Durand suddenly felt a sharp sting at the back of his right arm.

It took a second or two to pivot around in the crush of people, but all he saw behind him was a sea of diverse faces wearing LFP glasses, pushing relentlessly forward and past him, headed toward the station entrance. No one reacted to his stare.

Durand tugged at the back of his jacket sleeve but could see nothing. The pain was still there. In fact, it was getting worse.

Shit.

He recalled reading an Interpol report a few months back on jabstick attacks in dense crowds—that they could happen right in front of security cameras without revealing the perpetrator. Psychologists theorized it was a form of rebellion against ubiquitous surveillance. Durand didn't recall any of the incidents occurring in Singapore, though.

He started to doubt himself. But damn, his arm hurt.

Durand struggled across the river of commuters to get to the nearest wall. Just downstream of a support pillar, he took off his suit jacket and checked the back of his shirtsleeve.

A spot of blood soaked through the synthetic silk.

He felt adrenaline surge. *Shit . . .*

Someone in the crowd had stabbed him. An accident? A random psycho? But then Durand realized he could feel more than just adrenaline. He recalled the first time he'd experienced a mortar attack in a CLU at Camp Lemonnier. Alarms wailing as thumps rattled the walls. *That* was adrenaline.

This was something else.

The urge to vomit. Trembling hands, yes. But something else was coursing through him, too. A burning sensation. He could feel it spreading. Was it psychosomatic?

I haven't been stabbed—I've been injected.

An injection under high pressure.

The Huli jing use synbiotoxins.

That's what Marcotte had said. Wasn't that what she'd said? He needed to get help.

Durand tried to tap his LFP glasses to instantiate a phone—but his arm muscles had begun to spasm. The more he tried to move them, the more disconnected they seemed to become. And then he noticed his fingers were swelling.

He tried to speak to his virtual assistant, but his tongue didn't obey him, either—it was swelling fast. His throat constricted.

Durand staggered out into the flood of passing commuters. He stepped in front of them, pleading wordlessly. Workers pushed past him as he howled at them for help, raising a swelling hand. He began to drool uncontrollably, his face suddenly numb. His muscles began to clench in excruciating spasms, causing him to call out in pain.

The commuters looked away—intent on their own lives and virtual interactions. Not wanting to get involved in his reality.

Durand looked up at the ceiling and parapets around and above him—where he knew security cameras would be. But in this precise spot, he could see none.

That's not a coincidence.

Only then did he realize just how well planned this had been.

Durand pitched forward and collapsed onto the concrete floor. He rolled onto his back, staring upward at the graceful, arched ceiling of the wet market.

Passing commuters finally reacted, shouting in several languages, edging around him, some holding the crowd back so he didn't get trampled.

Durand's throat continued to constrict. He struggled for air. Looking up at the concerned faces all around him, he could tell by their expressions that he was in trouble. He could feel the skin of his face tightening.

Someone had intentionally injected him. *The Huli jing use synbiotoxins.* He recalled the gallery of dead.

Still clutching his daughter's gift with a paralyzed arm, he struggled to raise his free hand. His fingers were now so badly swollen that his wedding ring had become a tourniquet.

A group of commuters cleared space around Durand, shouting. Curious onlookers knotted around the scene.

"Call ambulance, lah!"

"Serangan jantung?"

"Mite, sugoku hareteiru!"

"Stay back! He looks contagious!"

Durand stared at people's feet. So many expensive shoes. Sneakers were not popular in Singapore. His breathing became more and more labored. Men knelt close to him, loosening his tie, unbuttoning his shirt.

"Usake paas se door hato!"

Durand soon became aware of uniformed paramedics arriving. They wore visored helmets. One of them leaned in close, checking Durand's vitals.

Durand tried to speak, but his swollen tongue and constricted throat rendered him mute.

Mia and Miyuki would be so disappointed. His mother, too. She'd never wanted him to travel here. Durand also realized how disappointed he was. He closed his eyes and concentrated.

Please, not this way. Not now.

Radio chatter in an unknown language. The whole world was looking and sounding strange now. Distorted. Leering faces of professional men and women.

He couldn't move. His entire body was swollen in a violent reaction to something. His shirtsleeves and shoes squeezed him mercilessly. Unbearable muscle spasms increased. He groaned.

One paramedic pried the birthday gift from Durand's frozen arm. Durand's eyes tried to follow it, only to see the other paramedic lift metal clippers to Durand's hand—and snip the wedding band off of Durand's swollen index finger, leaving a red indentation where it had been choking off blood flow.

A toy poodle in the arms of a nearby elderly Chinese man started barking madly—and then struggled to escape as if in terror. It hopped out of the man's hands and fled between the feet of onlookers. The man shouted after it.

Durand watched reality with increasing detachment, his eyes wandering across the faces in the crowd above him. Then his eyes focused on one face just now leaning in close to his own—a handsome young Eurasian man. He wore a fine suit and had midlength black hair. He knelt just two feet away, gazing down, with both hands leaning on the engraved ivory handle of a full-length black umbrella. The double-Windsor knot of the man's pale yellow silk tie was perfect.

Durand stared into the young man's gray eyes.

They stared back with unflinching intensity.

Even though Durand struggled for air, his entire focus held on the young man. Though every way normal in appearance—refined even—an uncanny-valley effect pervaded him. The young man did not seem real. Some instinct screamed to Durand that the eyes regarding him were empty.

He felt growing terror as the man leaned even closer now, reaching across Durand. Every cell in Durand's body recoiled.

The young man picked up Mia's gift and tucked it underneath his own arm. With that, he drew back again to stare once more into Durand's eyes.

Durand could not turn away. Those cold gray eyes held him. He couldn't recall *ever* having seen eyes like that before. Unliving eyes. They watched as Durand's vision faded into darkness as an internal fire consumed him.

He could not even gather the breath to scream.

Chapter 6

Kenneth Durand knows it is August 2035. That already happened, but that's okay because it's a beautiful day. He's younger—in his midtwenties. O-3, Lieutenant Durand, on ten days' leave, walking in civilian clothes through the newly expanded Greenfield Terminal of Nairobi's Jomo Kenyatta International Airport alongside a younger *Sowi* Michael Yi Ji-chang. Yi frowns as he pokes at an actual handheld smartphone. They move through the busy terminal, dodging between Chinese businessmen and tourists. Durand's stride is easy and relaxed—though he has no reason to be relaxed.

"Ken, this connection's going to be frickin' tight." Yi motions for them to step it up.

They're catching a Safarilink flight from Wilson Airport to Amboseli—half a dozen other squad mates will be trying to hold the plane for them. They have yet to collect their bags, deal with customs, taxi across town.

Durand just cannot work up anxiety over it. He's not sure if that's the way he felt at the time. He suspects not. This trip was important to him. He bought an actual camera for this trip. Kilimanjaro. The game preserve. It all seemed really special. And it was special.

But not today.

They're pushing through the crowd at baggage claim. Durand sees his bag before Yi spots his own. Durand reaches for the handle at the same time that a young Japanese woman does.

She looks up in surprise as they brush hands. "This one's mine."

"American." It is an odd thing for him to say.

"Yes. And this is my bag."

Durand lets go. He looks down and realizes she's right. There's a bright red, embossed metal tag on it, held fast by a beaded chain. It's otherwise identical to his own bag—a matte black carbon fiber shell with the closest thing to off-road wheels. You could probably row the damn thing down the Nile. Now he sees his own bag coming up not far behind on the carousel. He points. "You have good taste."

She laughs.

He collects his bag. It is a highly practical bag. Only attractive for what it can do. Both their bags are scuffed from rough handling.

She telescopes the handle on hers and rolls it away—but only far enough to get clear of the crowd. She takes out a tablet and starts reconnecting with her world.

A glance. Yi still anxiously awaits the appearance of his own bag on the carousel.

Durand turns back. He studies the young woman. She is dressed for travel. Sensible shoes. Lots of pockets. She is not a tourist. She has been here many times before. He rolls up to her. "I have to ask."

She looks up from her tablet, her expression guarded.

"That's a serious bag."

"That's not a question."

"You must have a serious job."

"I do." She nods toward his bag. "And you?"

"Too serious. I've been considering a change. But then I'd have to give up the bag."

She laughs again. Her eyes smile.

The connecting flight is suddenly not so important. "You're arriving from where?"

"Far away."

"I've been there."

She points at her tablet. "I've got to get my drilling robots clear of customs, and then I'm headed to Mombasa with my project team. So . . ."

"Right. I'm meeting friends, too." He moves away and then circles back after going just a few meters. "But here's the thing: I'll be on the coast at the end of this week, and there's this great place on Diani Beach."

"Ali Barbour's Cave."

He laughs. "Right."

"I love that place."

"There's lots of people there. Come join me."

"I'll still be with my project team."

"Bring them. I'll take your whole damn project team out to dinner if it means you'll say yes."

She laughs again. He could get lost in her eyes. "There's a fine line between persistence and harassment."

He nods, a slight smile on his face. "There is. But this is probably the only time our paths will ever cross. Unless I ask you." He searches her eyes. "So I'm asking you."

She eyes him back. "Do you have a name?"

"I do." He extends his hand. "Ken Durand."

She shakes his hand with a firm grip. She has calluses on her hands. "Okay, Ken Durand. I'm Miyuki Uchida."

"Miyuki. Good to meet you."

And it was true. He knew it the moment he first saw her.

Chapter 7

Kenneth Durand found himself staring at a soft white light. It took a long while to focus well enough to discern the frame around it.

A ceiling light fixture.

He then slowly resolved the ceiling tiles around that. Eventually he cast his gaze downward and saw that he was in a modern intensive care unit—medical machines beeping and pumps hissing.

What the hell?

His entire body was racked by dull pain, as though he'd pulled every muscle. He noticed that he was wearing a hospital gown. An IV ran into his arm and a catheter into his groin. No blanket covered him—so he could plainly see the skin of his arms and legs bruised black, blue, and yellow.

Confusion clouded his mind, and he looked up to see sensors and medical equipment looming around his bed. He felt something lodged in his throat and tried to swallow around it awkwardly. Panic rose as his gag reflex kicked in—until he saw the breathing tube leading from his mouth to a nearby ventilator. It hissed rhythmically, soothingly, and he felt air flow into his lungs. He could feel medical tape around his mouth securing it in place.

Durand closed his eyes again and tried to center himself. To remain calm. He had no idea how he'd gotten here.

He heard *beep-beep*ing as his heart rate settled once more. He opened his eyes and looked around the ICU. His bed was partitioned on the left and right by sliding curtains. He didn't hear any movement or talking beyond them, just the hisses of machines.

But then he discerned the whine of an approaching electric motor. A boxy wheeled robot soon came into view, emblazoned with a red cross. It rolled to a stop at the foot of his hospital bed, then turned to face him. A soft voice emanated from it as a soothing blue light pulsed: *"Please be calm. I have summoned assistance. Sila bertenang. Saya telah memanggil bantuan . . ."*

Durand focused on the pulsing pastel blue light and found it reassuring. He wondered what psychological research had led to its deployment. He decided the research was solid because he did feel soothed by its glowing, then fading—like waves lapping a beach. He had no idea what the hell was going on, but this machine apparently did, and that was some consolation.

Moments later an Indian woman doctor assisted by a Hoklo male nurse arrived to check Durand's vitals. The doctor tested Durand's pupils with a penlight. Satisfied, she looked closely at him and spoke in British-accented English. "Can you hear me?"

Durand nodded.

"I am Dr. Chaudhri." She placed a reassuring hand on Durand's shoulder. "You've been in a coma. Do you understand?"

The news hit Durand hard. After a moment or two of panic, he nodded slowly, despite the tubes leading from his throat.

The doctor squeezed Durand's shoulder again. "You've suffered a massive allergic reaction to something—we don't yet know what. However, we believe you're out of danger. Still, we're going to keep you in the ICU for a little while longer."

Durand studied his bruised and bandaged arms and hands. They looked almost alien.

The doctor followed his gaze. "The swelling receded only yesterday."

On Durand's effort to speak the doctor said, "I'm going to remove your breathing tube. Please just relax. This will not hurt, though it will be briefly uncomfortable."

The nurse moved in to assist, and after they removed the medical tape, Durand felt an alarmingly long tube snake out of his throat. He gagged a bit as the last of it came out, and felt again a dreadful soreness in his stomach muscles, ribs, and chest as he coughed. The agonizing coughing fit continued for several seconds.

The doctor's soothing hand was on his shoulder again. "You're safe now, but your heart stopped for a bit last week." She smiled. "You're quite the fighter."

With the tubes out Durand croaked, "How long have I been here?" His voice sounded as awful as his throat felt.

"Almost five weeks."

Five weeks? That was impossible. He'd just been talking with colleagues at the GCI. What happened? He looked back up at her. "What hospital?"

"Mount Elizabeth."

Durand stared blankly.

"Mount Elizabeth Hospital, Singapore. You were found without identification. Can you tell me your name?"

Durand struggled to process all this news. *Without identification?*

The doctor repeated, "You were found without identification. Do you remember your name?"

He took a deep breath. "I'm Kenneth Andrew Durand. Lead geospatial analyst with Interpol GCI. I'm a US citizen."

The doctor took notes on a totem device—an inert physical object commonly used as a handy surface on which to interact with virtual screens. "You're with Interpol?"

He nodded. "I don't know how I got here. Where are my wife and daughter? Are they okay?"

The doctor took additional notes. "You were found alone and unconscious in a stolen car parked in Boon Lay."

"Boon Lay?"

"Were you with your wife and daughter?"

Durand shook his head absently, recalling that he hadn't been. "No. No, they weren't with me." He wasn't quite sure how he knew that. But he did. He looked up. "I've been here five weeks?"

She nodded.

He struggled to understand. "No one came looking for me?"

"The police came."

"Police? Why didn't they contact my family? Or contact Interpol?"

"No one could ID you."

Durand looked up at her incredulously. "That makes no sense."

"You're not in our national DNA registry. Now we know why: you're American."

"The American embassy should have been searching for me. Interpol. My family."

The doctor leaned close and spoke slowly. "Understand, Mr. Durand, we were initially concerned you'd been infected by a contagious pathogen—a hemorrhagic fever or new synbio organism. You were black with bruising—your entire body and face badly swollen. Your skin scabrous. Not even your ethnicity was apparent. Even your hair fell out. Yours has been a curious case."

"But . . . fingerprints."

She lifted his left hand and opened the palm toward him. He could see bandages wrapping his fingertips.

"The swelling split your skin at the extremities. It's still healing. Some required stitches."

Durand studied his bandaged fingers and now discerned the soreness underneath. He looked up at her.

"Your eyes hemorrhaged as well—so we couldn't scan your retinas. They're still alarming to behold. We've ruled out contagious disease, but we don't yet know what caused your body's violent reaction."

He searched for words. "My name is Kenneth Andrew Durand. I live in Woodlands with my wife, Miyuki Uchida, and our daughter, Mia." Durand got emotional. "I need to see them. They must be frantic." He paused. "It was my daughter's birthday."

"A birthday is the least of your concerns at the moment." The doctor touched his shoulder again. "I'll contact your wife immediately, Mr. Durand. Do you have a number I can call?"

"You don't have my phone? I . . ." He realized this, of course, must be the case. "I had no identification on me? Nothing?"

Forgiving of his disorientation, she shook her head.

He saw that even his wedding band was missing. "They took my wedding ring."

"Someone robbed you?"

He clutched his bandaged hand, but could clearly see the ring was gone. "I remember a young man with an umbrella . . . He was terrifying. And paramedics. I remember paramedics."

She stared back.

"My wife's number is 9-3-9-3-9-4-7-8-7."

She jotted it down. "You're safe now, Mr. Durand. We think you'll make a full recovery. Though we'll want to continue tests to pinpoint the source of your allergic response."

As she turned to go, Durand clutched at the hem of her coat with his bandaged hand. "Interpol. Please contact Interpol here in Singapore. Ask for Detective Inspector Claire Belanger. They need to know where I am. It's critically important."

"The number?"

He paused. Security protocols started to come back to him. "Call the main Interpol line here in Singapore. Tell them who I am, and they'll direct you."

"Inspector Claire Belanger." The doctor wrote the name down.

Durand felt suddenly exhausted.

The doctor moved his arm back onto the bed. "Get some rest, Mr. Durand. We'll contact the authorities and your family. Your job now is simply to get well."

He nodded weakly. "Thank you, Doctor."

She and the nurse departed.

Exhausted, Durand dozed off.

Durand awoke to the sound of someone clearing their throat. He looked up to see Inspector Claire Belanger and Sergeant Michael Yi Ji-chang standing at the foot of his hospital bed. Neither of their expressions looked particularly friendly.

Durand straightened in the bed. "Claire. Mike. Thank god." His voice sounded gravelly and hoarse.

They exchanged concerned looks and resumed staring.

Durand then noticed that he was no longer in the intensive care unit but in a private room. It was evening outside. He wondered how and when they'd moved his hospital bed, but then decided it didn't matter.

"I was poisoned." Even his tongue felt odd, making it difficult to sound out words. "A jab-stick in the middle of a crowd near the Tekka wet market. I think the Huli jing did it."

They said nothing.

"My comcar malfunctioned and dumped me near downtown. Somebody must have been following me. Which means we've had a security breach."

They still did not react.

"We should get techs down here to pull a blood sample. There might still be traces of the biotoxin they used in my system." He winced as he sat up slightly. "Also, Anna and Gus should do a pattern analysis on all telephone calls radiating out from my location immediately following the assassination attempt. Geolocation data on all comm devices in the area, too—and communities of interest going out two generations at least, one minute before and after, looking for echoes."

Belanger and Yi continued staring at him.

Durand pressed on. "And a protective detail. They tried to kill me once, they'll try again. I think the only reason I'm alive is because I was brought in here as a John Doe. And for god's sake, put a protective detail on Miyuki and Mia. Better yet, put them on a plane to the States. Her parents will be glad to see them."

Durand regarded the unfriendly eyes of his colleagues. "This is typically where you guys say how *great* it is to see me alive."

Neither of them did.

As he tried to lift his arm, Durand's wrist tugged back to the rattling of metal. He looked down to see that he was handcuffed to the bed rail. "What the hell . . . ?"

Yi moved toward the bed, pulling a document out of his jacket pocket as he approached. He unfolded the paper and dropped it into Durand's lap.

It was a familiar Interpol Red Notice—with text and DNA profile information and also the photo of a familiar, thuggish Eurasian man— labeled with the name Marcus Demang Wyckes.

"We know who you are, Mr. Wyckes. Matched your DNA. And we'd like to have a word with you regarding the whereabouts of Kenneth Durand."

Chapter 8

Inspector Belanger, Sergeant Yi, and Dr. Chaudhri stood in a radiology lab, examining a wall of virtual medical imagery on an AR layer shared through their LFP glasses. Floating before them were X-rays, 3D scans of bone structure, dental records, MRIs.

"Why didn't you confirm the patient's identity before contacting Durand's wife?"

Dr. Chaudhri cast an annoyed look Belanger's way. "I had no way of knowing who this man was. Not even the police could identify him."

Yi interceded. "She's right, Claire. The SPF must have gotten their samples mixed up. I came here last month hoping this guy was Ken—been to every hospital and morgue in Singapore and Johor a dozen times. City police gave me his DNA profile. I ran it through CODIS. No matches."

Belanger thought out loud. "And today—"

"I watched Dr. Chaudhri draw two different blood samples. Ran the GlobalFiler assay myself, and the DNA profiles were both perfect matches for Wyckes. I nearly fell over. The first test had to be a lab mix-up."

Belanger mused, "And the only reason we're here is because he claimed to be Ken. Wyckes called us here himself."

Yi shrugged. "Strange, isn't it? For Wyckes to do that."

"There must be some reason." Belanger held up her hands. "Apologies for my ill temper, Dr. Chaudhri. But our missing agent's wife and daughter are more traumatized than ever by your call. I'll need to go see them."

had organometallic lights bright enough to trace its outline even in daytime.

The gull-wing limo door rose automatically. Otto emerged into the sunlight. He wore a well-tailored gray suit. His pastel pink double-Windsor knot, as always, perfect. He might not choose his face, but he carefully chose his wardrobe.

Otto mounted wide marble steps, atop which stood uniformed, heavily armed soldiers of indeterminate Central Asian nationality and ethnicity. They bore no insignias or unit patches on their randomized, digitally printed urban camouflage uniforms. Were they Kazakh? Turkmen? Mongolian? It was difficult to know.

As he reached the top of the steps, a K-9 patrol passed on its circuit of the building. Two vicious mastiffs snarled and strained against their masters' leashes.

But as they drew near Otto, the dogs raised their ears, drew back, and then whimpered before straining with all their might to flee. Soon the soldiers were shouting commands as the dogs pulled free and fled in terror into the wide, empty street, yelping like puppies.

The feeling was mutual, as far as Otto was concerned. Animals were simply more honest than humans.

The entire line of soldiers avoided Otto's gaze, and glass doors hissed open to admit him into a high-ceilinged lobby hung with ornate crystal chandeliers. The world's gaudiest gold-and-mirrored service robot vacuumed rich red carpets that were trimmed in gold tassels.

Otto trailed his hand affectionately over the robot's polished surface as he passed by. He had a soft spot for robots. They weren't as off-putting as humans.

He entered an elevator car paneled in mahogany, crystal, and brass. Without his selecting a floor, its doors closed and whisked him to the penthouse. There, Otto exited, walking between grim security men in blue suits bulging from gel body armor. The final two guards stood before closed oak doors richly carved with Asian dragon motifs.

The guard on the left, a six-foot-eight, bearded mountain of a man, held his hand up to stop Otto. "He's in a private meeting, Mr. Otto. He asked not to be disturbed."

Otto let a crooked smile crease his face. He then walked right up to the guard while the man's colleague gazed nervously elsewhere. Otto held out his hand as if to shake. "And who are you?"

Uncertain, the first guard extended his own massive hand. "I'm—"

Otto swiftly clasped the guard's hand, watching closely as a sheen of sweat appeared almost immediately on the guard's face. Seconds later a dark wet stain spread from the guard's crotch, urine dripping onto his dress shoes.

The man pulled free from Otto's grip and backed away from the door—and then away from Otto entirely. Existential dread was written on his face. He gasped for air. "I'm sorry. I'm sorry! Please . . ."

The other guard swung the doors open without a word, still avoiding Otto's gaze.

Otto calmly entered the penthouse office. It had a sweeping view of the unpopulated city below. The double doors closed behind him.

He heard voices to his right and turned to see an Indian bioengineer in a white lab coat speaking to the owner of the office—who stood with his back turned inside a large, ornately fashioned conservatory. The enclosure was alive with fluttering silver, black, white, and orange butterflies and was easily twenty feet wide. It contained potted trees, a fountain, and flowers.

Otto would recognize Marcus Wyckes anywhere by his commanding presence. He didn't need to see the man's face. In fact, Wyckes's face, like Otto's, was forever changing. But Wyckes's presence never changed. And it was why this human was the closest thing to a father that Otto would ever have.

Otto approached silently.

The researcher spoke haltingly to Wyckes. "We did as instructed . . . prepared a . . . a lethal change agent . . . a revision to your birth DNA."

Wyckes observed a silver-gold-and-black butterfly crawl across the back of his hand as he replied with an Australian accent, "I didn't instruct you to include my chromatophores. Now this man apparently has my unique mark of rank. He's already displayed it in public."

The bioengineer stammered. "We . . . we have never performed a lethal transformation outside this facility, Master Wyckes. And it has never been raised as an issue before."

Wyckes's voice remained calm. "Was I born with chromatophores?"

"No. Of course, you were not, Master Wyckes. But I assumed you wanted him to be mistaken for you."

"*After* he was dead—not *before* he was dead."

"But, Master Wyckes, the added processing to remove chromatophores would have been—"

As Otto quietly came alongside the researcher, the man drew back as if he sensed something *wrong* nearby.

The butterflies within the conservatory suddenly took flight en masse, fluttering from the back of Wyckes's hand. Every one of them clustered at the farthest point from Otto that they could manage.

Wyckes spoke without turning. "Otto." He turned and smiled, revealing a mix of Slavic and Chinese features—ruddy-faced with short black hair. He wore a cashmere sweater and tailored slacks. "Humanity's last hope has returned."

Otto smiled slightly.

Wyckes nodded to the researcher. "Leave us."

The man happily complied, clearly eager to get away from Otto.

Otto opened the conservatory door for Wyckes. They did not touch as Wyckes exited, but Wyckes smiled warmly before moving toward a massive mahogany desk a dozen meters away, near the tall bank of windows. The desk was carved with Chinese dragon motifs and entirely out of keeping with the modern architecture of the office.

"I'm glad you're back so soon."

Otto's voice was measured. Calm. "Our new partners were very cooperative."

"Well, that's fortunate, because a problem has come up that requires your unique talents." Wyckes sat in an ancient-looking leather wing chair.

Otto sat in one of the two modern guest chairs in front of the desk, unbuttoning his suit jacket.

"Do you recall administering a very important injection for me in

Singapore last month? Into the Interpol agent responsible for locating so many of our partner labs?"

Otto considered the question for a moment, then nodded. "Yes. In a crowded train station, I recall."

Wyckes nodded. "Yes. The dose was meant to be a lethal change agent to transform the man into someone very special: me."

Otto contemplated the event. "That was uncomfortable—being among so many humans."

Wyckes's expression softened. "You know how much I appreciate your sacrifices, Otto. Our research would not be possible without you."

"Has there been a complication?"

"Yes. Unfortunately, the target did not perish after the transformation completed. He survived. And what's worse, he's now running around loose."

Otto pondered this news. "As you?"

Wyckes shrugged. "As what I once was. At least partially so. And worse still, he's got this . . ."

With that, a full complement of green, blue, black, and orange tattoos faded into existence on Wyckes's neck, forearms, and knuckles. Within seconds they stood out in vibrant color. From a mild-seeming businessman, he now had the appearance of an arch Yakuza or Triad warlord.

As if by reflex, Otto's chromatophores responded in kind. He saw his own Huli jing tattoos surface on his hands, but knew they were activated across his chest, back, arms, neck, and legs, too.

They both had unique patterns. Their own signature.

Otto nodded. "Your marks of rank. That is a problem."

Wyckes nodded back. "Yes. It's a problem. One I need you to resolve." He made several hand gestures and a desk-mounted LFP beamed virtual images into Otto's retinas.

Internet newsfeeds floated before Otto. One headline read, "Cartel Kingpin Kills Officers in Dramatic Escape," with a scan of police boots sticking out of an elevator door. The other article showed an Interpol Red Notice and photo of a bald, fierce-looking man that in no way resembled the Marcus Wyckes sitting in front of him. That headline read: "Infamous Gangster Loose in Singapore."

Wyckes nodded toward the images. "I'm not sure how he did it, but this Interpol agent is now on the run. Our friends in the police failed to do their job."

"Will they find him?"

"We can no longer rely on the police. But the media should make it easier to locate this person. His face—that is, my old face—is all over the news. I'm now wanted in nearly two hundred countries. It'll be difficult for him to hide." Wyckes passed the virtual Interpol Red Notice to Otto—who examined the image carefully.

"I want you to do what the police could not: find this imposter, kill him, and leave his body where it'll be quickly found by the authorities. It's high time for Marcus Demang Wyckes to finally die—and his lengthy criminal record along with him."

Otto nodded. "It also eliminates our most troublesome enemy. There is a beautiful symmetry to your plan. I will see it done."

"Good." Wyckes smiled, closing his eyes in relief. "I knew I could count on you, Otto. You know there is no one I trust more in this entire doomed world than you."

Otto stood, and with a nod, he headed for the elevator.

Chapter 15

The junkie's phablet was cheap, Tanzanian-made shit. And Kenneth Durand wasn't used to tapping at a physical screen as he walked. AR light field displays were a much more natural way to interact with information. But then nonretinal displays had huge advantages to criminals (which Durand now technically was); they couldn't easily rat you out.

Durand had been walking for several kilometers down a long drainage channel, headed northward. Holding up the phablet screen and comparing his location to a city map, he turned down the next side tunnel and edged around motion sensors, lowering his head as he passed a camera.

These, too, appeared to be out of commission. It was obvious that the criminal element moving about the tunnel system beneath the city regularly broke the devices and sabotaged locked entry gates—although the locks were disguised to appear intact. Durand was surprised the SPF tolerated this. He remembered all the security data being fed into his systems from Singapore officials, and he wondered to what degree any of it was true. He found it hard to believe that Singapore would tolerate malfunctioning motion sensors and bent gates in a drainage channel going out to the Strait—allowing passage by random people unchecked. How could they permit junkies and transients to wander across the city unobserved via the drainage channels?

He wondered if this was a state of affairs Michael Yi would recognize. Had the SPF relegated security to informers among the junkie population? Had they come to terms with criminal gangs to keep an eye out for terrorists moving through? Human intelligence was something streets cops infinitely preferred to IoT data.

Durand was starting to realize they might have a point.

He passed by a couple of Filipino teens strutting to Thai retro-funk. The music echoed confidently in the tunnel, but the young men turned their music down and moved warily around Durand on the far side of the tunnel as he glared at them. They looked petrified. Urban explorers? Future synth addicts? Difficult to say.

Durand made sure the teens didn't double-back on him, and then, referencing the phablet map again, he turned down a side passage that ended in a steel gate with a thick lock built into it and menacing-looking alarms. Beyond it, he could see MRT rails and diamond-plate stairs. He pushed against the locked gate, and it came open, as the previous ones had—maximum-security appearance notwithstanding.

In a moment, Durand moved up the maintenance stairs and found himself walking on a catwalk alongside an MRT subway track. Up ahead there was another gate, and he could see bright lighting with commuters and transit police moving on a station platform.

There would be working cameras here, so he inserted phablet-linked earphones, tossed the camouflage jacket, and pulled up the hoodie on his sweatshirt. He then flipped his phablet screen to anime he'd found in its library—no doubt torrented. He turned the volume to zero, then pushed through the maintenance gate and let it close behind him with a bang—as if he didn't give a damn who saw him.

He moved out onto the subway platform with other commuters, head bobbing to imaginary music as the cartoon titles played.

Woodlands station—his MRT stop. He wasn't far from home now.

He kept his head down, ostensibly engrossed in the animation as he passed what he knew were numerous surveillance cameras—running real-time facial recognition in a photonic cloud.

But Durand knew more than most people about these systems—knew what they were and were not capable of. He also knew what the algorithms were searching for. Loitering, rapid movements, recognizable weapons—all of these set off alarm bells. So did positive matches for wanted felons— particularly those who'd been headscanned, like he'd been. However, an overreliance on automated systems meant that second-order anomalies weren't caught; whereas a human might think it odd that someone was wearing a sweatshirt with the hood up on a warm day, algorithms weren't yet sharp enough to connect those dots—at least not the systems used by MRT security.

Durand also knew it was common for commuters to read and keep to themselves, avoiding eye contact with others as they pushed through the crowd. He tried to recall security conferences where vendors described what type of "suspicious behavior" their algorithms looked for.

Durand headed up the stairs to street level. Two transit police passed by him, and he laughed to an imaginary phone companion, turning away. He was relieved when they paid no attention to him.

Durand reached daylight. It was wonderful to be in fresh air again, partly sunny and in the midseventies. To smell familiar smells. He kept his head down, but activated the phablet's front-facing camera as a form of periscope—allowing him to look ahead without lifting his face to street-level surveillance cameras. He knew there were camera pods on every sign pole and streetlight in this neighborhood. It had been a selling point actually.

He angled the phablet across Woodlands Terrace road, revealing the six eighty-story towers of the Hanging Gardens complex where he lived, linked at their summit by a ring of greenery. The Woodlands district was popular with expats and biotech folk. The neighborhood was a showroom for the built environment. And its security infrastructure was also constantly searching for trouble.

As he crossed the street, it only just now occurred to Durand that the prior owner of the phablet might have problems that would flag him as trouble to local police. Had the man ever been arrested? Was he a known synth addict?

The analyst in him tried to derive what Singapore's algorithms might be watching for in his neighborhood. Durand hoped that walking head-down, gazing at a *physical* device, wasn't going to make algorithms suspicious of him as a low-rent invader. And yet someone walking facedown could be looking at a map or having a conversation with a child or eating. There would be just too many errors on a typical crowded street to react to them all. It was one of the reasons why automated facial recognition systems were imperfect at best—why so many other data points needed to be cross-referenced to identify people: their phone IDs, the NFC chips in their credit fobs, Bluetooth IDs, and a dozen other technological tracers. IoT data frequently overwhelmed authorities.

None of these currently connected this device to Wyckes—and Wyckes was the one everyone was looking for, hopefully elsewhere (like at the border).

Durand passed by his own building and surreptitiously viewed the lobby through his phablet camera. He could see no additional police presence in front of the building or inside.

This actually made him angry. There should have been a security detail guarding his family.

Though, of course, Interpol had no police powers to provide one. And he'd been missing over a month.

Maybe Miyuki had taken Mia back to her parents' home in Chicago. He felt a pang of homesickness but also relief at the thought of their being out of harm's way.

Durand, on the other hand, needed to get into his flat, and precisely how he was going to do it without getting arrested (or, more likely, killed) was an open question.

There was a rear service entrance to his building. He'd cleared the delivery of their new refrigerator through there a year ago. Durand walked purposefully around the block and turned down the side street, passing the building's service alley. An elevator company service truck was parked some ways down the alley, as were a couple dozen electric scooters—probably from domestic workers. Nannies. Maids. Tradesmen and domestic help went in and out of his building all the time. As he glanced at the service entrance, a young Filipina maid walked out, obviously poking at a virtual screen to catch up on messages.

It occurred to Durand that although his building used biometrics—analyses of face, walk, voice, and a dozen other traits—to recognize flat owners, biometric recognition didn't actually grant access; it just made the building polite, allowing it to greet tenants by name and make them feel cared for. It was actually a chip in a key fob that granted access to the building. If someone the building did not recognize tried to gain access with a key fob, it would alert human security, but could also still grant access. People had guests all the time, and operationally it was just too difficult to manage all the exceptions.

Plus, biometrics had fallen into disfavor back in the 2020s. Once spoofed by a hacker, they were burned, and an individual couldn't very well invalidate their own retinas and get new ones (with the sole exception of Durand perhaps). So instead, biometrics were used in combination with revocable credentials—fobs, chips, passcodes, and one-time codes. A whole mix.

Which meant he actually had a way of granting himself access to his building: he could schedule a service call through the concierge console. All residents had an account.

It took him a while to search out the landing page with the phablet—particularly since he wasn't familiar with older, two-dimensional browsers. His first login attempt failed, but he guessed right on the second try (and confirmed why passwords were so awful from a security point of view). The scheduling screen came up, and he navigated to a grid showing the maid's schedule. He noticed there was a cat nanny listed as well, arriving daily in the midafternoon. A cat nanny—had Miyuki and Mia indeed headed for the States? Quarantine would have prevented them from taking Nelson, so it made sense.

Durand felt horrible for his daughter. First losing her father, and then parting with her toyger. But then he realized the more time he stood here, the more likely he was to appear suspicious.

Checking the time, Durand noticed the cat nanny's visit was only a couple of hours from now. He tapped at the physical screen awkwardly but managed to create an appointment for an electrician just a few minutes after the nanny. He typed in a fictitious name.

Roderick Feines.

Good enough. Durand walked a few blocks away on side streets, occasionally stepping aside to use the phablet to search online for uniforms, tools—everything he needed. Singapore was the global capital of same-day drone delivery, and "current location" was always a delivery option. Lots of expats worked out of coffeehouses and cocktail bars these days. Tradesmen on job sites. It shouldn't raise any red flags, and Durand still had quite a few bitrings on him for payment.

Food!

Durand suddenly realized just how hungry he was. He hadn't had solid food in over a month. Best to start with liquid nourishment since his digestive system would need time to restart. He checked the time again and then searched for a local juicing kiosk that offered drone delivery.

A couple hours later, Durand entered through the service entrance at the back of his home building wearing a new work shirt, boots, and work pants and holding an electrician's toolbox. A brand-new olive drab cap shielded his face from most of the cameras as he looked for his business card.

He nodded to the security guard and signed in. The guard checked to confirm Durand was expected and provided a visitor's fob that granted access to the floor that had requested him—and only for the scheduled time. The guard absently told Durand to use the service elevator.

In a few moments, Durand was at the fifty-sixth floor. He exited into familiar environs from an unfamiliar direction. The building didn't bid him good afternoon—and neither did one of his passing neighbors, Raz, an Indian geneticist in his thirties who worked from home. There wasn't a hint of recognition in the man's face.

Good.

Durand walked past the door to his own flat without seeing any additional police presence. He then pulled out and studied his phablet diligently—appearing busy.

In a couple of minutes he heard his flat door open behind him. But what he heard next set his heart racing . . .

Miyuki's voice.

She sounded tired and stressed as she told someone, "The vet information is on the cupboard door. With the food."

A young woman with a Malay accent answered, "But I need feeding information—"

"I . . . I'm sorry. I can send it to you. I'm not normally this disorganized. I'm sorry."

Durand turned toward them, still holding the phablet in his hand. He froze as he caught sight of his wife just meters away. Her eyes looked puffy, and he instantly knew she'd been crying. She'd received false hope about her husband just yesterday.

"What do you do?" A little girl's voice—one Durand would recognize in utter darkness.

Durand looked down at his six-year-old daughter, Mia, staring at him from near her mother. They both pulled rolling luggage behind them.

They were leaving.

Seeing the complete lack of recognition in his own daughter's eyes, Durand felt further away from them than ever before—even though they were right here in front of him. This was everything he'd been hoping for, but now that he was here—he could not come back to them like this. Not this way.

His daughter gave him a quizzical look.

Durand cleared his throat. "I'm the electrician."

Mia pointed at him and looked at her mother as she smiled. "Cooool."

Miyuki looked to the nanny. "We have to go. I will send you a message with all the information." She glanced down. "Mia, please stop bothering that man. Inspector Belanger is waiting for us." Miyuki placed a hand on her daughter's head, and they both moved toward the elevators.

Durand watched them go, on the verge of chasing after them. But to what point? To terrify them? He noticed the hand holding the phablet now bore his tattoo-like markings again. He tugged up his sleeve and saw that they continued up his arm. The deep emotion he felt at this moment had caused them to reappear. This much he now knew. There was a logic to them, then.

He looked up to see his wife and daughter enter the elevator. His daughter stared back. She waved, nearly crushing him.

And then the doors closed.

Durand stood in the corridor alone, only then noticing that the cat nanny had reentered the apartment. Gathering his resolve, he approached his flat door to knock, but just then it reopened. He ducked to the side as the young woman exited. He could hear her music playing in head-phones, and she was already engrossed in her LFP glasses as she walked down the corridor, also headed to the elevators.

Durand lunged toward the door, managing to catch the lever handle just before it shut. He then slipped inside.

The alarm was *BEEP-BEEP*ING, but he tapped the disarm code into the keypad—glad that he hadn't had the old physical interface removed. Durand felt tremendous relief when his own front door latched closed behind him.

He looked around his living room, and then over to his wife's office, with its glass wall. Her desk was cleared off. The photos on her back wall gone.

The place felt emotionally empty. Glancing into the kitchen, he could see that the photos and 3D-printed models were gone from the refrigerator door as well. There was fresh food and water for the cat, but no other sign of recent habitation.

Miyuki had taken Mia and gone somewhere with Inspector Belanger. Durand was relieved. They hadn't moved, but clearly they weren't stay-ing here anymore.

He was glad they were somewhere safe—with someone who loved Mia almost as much as he did. He had to take care of this impossible situation.

He moved through the dining room and past the laundry room. Durand passed by his daughter's bedroom and nudged the door open.

Her solar system mobile and horse-themed comforter were still in place. But the room was much neater than it normally was. Her desk, too, was immaculate—something that had never happened before.

Durand restored the door to its previous, half-opened position, and then entered his own bedroom. He closed his eyes and inhaled deeply. The familiar scents brought powerful memories of who he was—of Miyuki lying next to him in the darkness.

He turned to see a framed photograph on their bureau dresser—of his real self smiling with his wife and daughter at Hong Kong Disney-land. Durand picked up the photo frame and touched it with alien fingers. He looked up at the strange reflection in his own bedroom mirror. Perhaps the face of the man who had done this to him.

Desperation began to resurface. Was there any hope of getting back? Was he just kidding himself? Kenneth Durand was gone.

He was startled by his daughter's toyger, Lord Nelson, leaping up onto the bureau dresser. "Nelson . . . you scared the shit out of me."

Durand slumped in relief as the cat rubbed against his hand, purring loudly. Durand put the photo frame down and picked Nelson up, lifting him to his face while holding him under his forelegs. The toyger bumped his head affectionately against Durand's nose.

Durand sat down on the edge of the bed, nestling his daughter's cat close. "Nelson, Nelson."

There was still some of his original self left to detect apparently. There was still hope. He hugged the cat for the first time and then held him up to look him in the eyes. "Thanks, buddy. I really needed that."

He gently placed Nelson on the bed.

He had urgent business to attend to here. Durand went to the kitchen and retrieved small, resealable plastic baggies. He then entered the master bathroom and carefully retrieved strands of his own hair from his hairbrush and electric razor—looking especially for strands with the root. He sealed all the individual bags into a larger one.

Lord Nelson sat on the bathroom counter, observing impassively. Durand had never been happier to have the cat's company. "If I ever complain about you again, go ahead and scratch me."

Finally leveling a gaze at himself in his large bathroom mirror, Durand sighed deeply. He looked like hell. Aside from being a thuggish stranger, his face was bruised, and taking off his uniform, he could see the second-degree burn on his forearm from the hot cowling of the police drone.

Glancing at the shower, Durand decided there was no time like the present.

He took a long, hot soak, and felt relief cascade over him. He hurt all over, and the burn in particular was giving him trouble, but there was nothing like being home.

Once out of the shower, he glanced in the mirror at this new body. He'd never been physically intimidating—Durand had more of a runner's physique—but he now had a substantial chest, brawny arms, and a thick neck. He looked like some Eurasian middleweight wrestler. Looking more closely at his face, he was still amazed that his ethnicity had been changed. He was part Asian now.

He turned forward and back and could find no trace of the massive array of tattoos that had reappeared on him just minutes before. Strange. But then, that was the least strange thing that had happened to him lately.

He took out a first aid kit. The Naval Academy had drilled organization into him until it was habit. Durand knew where everything was in his flat, and it was well organized. He treated his burn with a synbio skin spray, then dressed his other wounds as best he could.

Looking back into the mirror, he was glad he was bald. He didn't want to see what Wyckes's hair would look like. From the shadow of growth forming, it was probably going to be black. His own hair was a dusty brown.

Durand entered the walk-in closet and could see that a portion of his wife's wardrobe was gone, along with her luggage. Durand couldn't help but wonder what her plan was. To get out of here for now, certainly, but what then?

He contemplated what he would have done if the reverse had happened—if one day his wife suddenly went missing. He realized it would consume him—even as he would have to care for Mia's well-being, too. He decided his wife had it tougher than he did right now.

Durand moved aside some of his suits. He felt closer to his real identity again, touching the synthetic gabardine, but felt a pang of melancholy when he discovered his dress shirts no longer fit—too narrow in the neck and shoulders.

Durand glanced at Nelson, who was shadowing him. He rubbed the cat under the chin. "Looks like we're going casual."

He put on one of his looser-fitting tracksuits and a pristine Colorado Rockies baseball hat.

Lastly, Durand went to the bureau dresser, where he took the family photo out of its frame. He examined the precious image of his wife, daughter, and finally his real self.

He *would* get back to his family—and to himself. He folded the photo and slipped it into his pocket. Durand then went into his wife's office and took one of her old-timey ink pens and quality vellum from a drawer where he knew she kept them. He glanced admiringly at her handwriting on a note there. It was something she did that he had always adored. Her writing was feminine and yet so confident—bold, graceful strokes.

His own handwriting was childish and crude—but then, he was a technology guy. As Durand lifted the pen, he wondered if his wife (or anyone) actually had a sample of his handwriting with which to confirm the authenticity of this note.

Durand placed the tip of the pen on paper, took a breath, and then wrote the following:

> *Dearest Miyuki and Mia,*
>
> *I am alive and safe for now—but as you probably guessed, I'm on the run from very bad people. You must stay away from home and in protective custody—preferably back in the United States. Ask Claire and Michael for help if you need it. Please tell my mother, brother, and sister that I love them. Do not try to look for me. I promise you, I will come back to you both. You are all that I live for.*
>
> > *Your loving husband and father,*
> > *Kenneth Durand*

Durand left the note against the empty photo frame in the bedroom. With one last look at the stranger in his own bedroom mirror, he pointed at his reflection.

"I'm coming for you, asshole."

With that, he exited his flat, and hoped it wasn't for the last time.

Chapter 16

Now equipped with proper exercise clothes, Kenneth Durand flipped up his hoodie and jogged as though he intended to work up a sweat in the humid heat.

The Singapore police were still looking for him, of course, but he knew where he needed to go. It was only a kilometer away. Durand aimed for the north waterfront and the line of farming towers covered in greenery. As he drew closer to the massive structures, he noticed aggie drones flitting around them like bees pollinating flowers.

The exterior of the towers was mostly public relations—displaying walls of flowering plants and supporting bee populations. But the real business was inside—highly productive, automated, aquaponic urban agriculture. Plants not visible from out here.

Soaked with sweat from his jog, Durand walked with an easy confidence toward the loading dock at the back of Farm Tower Four. It was owned by a company named Agriville—its logo a stylized flowering tree. Durand passed autonomous trucks and vans carrying racks of produce to local markets.

He nodded to a security guard in a shack near the rear gate. "Headed in to see Mr. Desai."

"Very well, please sign in, sir." He presented a ruggedized thirty-year-old tablet for Durand to sign.

Durand tapped in a random name on the visitor form and handed the device back. "I know where it is." He pushed through, and the bored security guard didn't object. Instead the man went back to watching something on a light field device.

Durand knew the route inside well enough, and he knew how to act among the very few human workers on the ground floor. He moved immediately toward a shipping clerk's office and reached inside the open doorway. Without looking, he pulled a yellow composite hard hat from a rack next to the door. He also grabbed an ID badge on a lanyard from an unlocked locker and looped it around his neck. The photo on it distracted him momentarily—it showed his old self above the name Martin Peele.

Durand then grabbed a work tablet and headed toward the large freight elevators. Autonomous forklifts moved pallets of produce to and fro, their warning lights flashing. He entered the elevator and watched as the button panel turned green to show he had access. Durand tapped the button for the seventy-fifth floor.

As the open elevator car rose, he saw floor after floor of purplish light illuminating endless racks of lush, highly diverse plants. Purple was a frequency of artificial sunlight alien to human eyes, but divine to plants. Here, Agriville grew produce to order for restaurants and markets all over the city, with the entire operation managed by a data-driven logistics system. Each row and each shelf might grow a hundred different plants for a dozen different clients. Or a single client. Specialized, track-mounted robots managed seed retrieval, planting, germination, and plant care.

As the floors zoomed past, Durand saw only one or two human beings moving about—monitoring autonomous operations mostly. On the whole, the entire facility and the surrounding towers just like it were almost completely automated. Not many people necessary, really. That created opportunities for the more enterprising.

Durand glanced back at the impressive skyline behind him—Johor Bahru across the Strait. Autonomous ships plied the water. Security drones patrolled the coast. He had no doubt the search for Wyckes was still in full swing—that they were expecting Wyckes to flee the country. To get back to his people.

The elevator came to a stop with a loud musical tone that could be heard halfway across the rack-filled floor. Durand exited and moved with purpose along the wide aisle at the head of the racks, glancing at the numbers.

At aisle forty-two, he turned in, squeezing past several robots that rolled past on rails built into the shelving. They sprayed water, pruned leaves, and searched for blights and parasites with microscopic care.

Durand walked a hundred meters to the end of the aisle, where he saw a cage door with no markings. He approached with his head down, eyes on the ruggedized tablet, knowing full well there was a camera watching the doorway. As he reached the gate, he raised his ID badge up to the lens.

The gate clicked open and Durand pushed through. The metal cage slammed behind him as he slipped next through a fire-rated security door marked with a biohazard symbol and the text "Danger" in multiple languages.

Durand entered a space where classical music played on hidden speakers. As the door eased shut behind him, he surveyed a sprawling laboratory where white lab robots holding racks of microtubes rolled past on rubber wheels. Centrifuges whirred, their payloads a blur. Cooling fans of DNA-sequencing machines hummed. This place was noticeably cleaner and more technical than elsewhere in the building.

Durand walked past flowering plants growing in the shape of company logos or broad tropical leaves bearing advertising slogans. He nudged past another potted plant bearing juice boxes as fruit, replete with branded packaging, scan codes, and ingredients listed on their biodegradable skin.

This was, in fact, an illegal embryo-editing lab—albeit one for making illegal edits to plants.

Staring via LFP glasses into the virtual screen of an advanced-looking microscope, Malaysian geneticist Radheya Desai sat on a lab stool, his back to Durand. The man was slightly overweight, balding, and wore a white lab coat. Without turning, Desai held up a rubber-gloved hand. "Marty. I'll be with you in a moment."

The classical music continued to play.

Durand cleared his throat and tossed his hard hat onto a nearby counter. "Rad, I need your help."

Desai turned in alarm, his face registering fear at the sight of this burly stranger in his lab. "Shit." He killed the music with a wave of his hand. In the silence he glanced over at a wall-mounted alarm button several meters away.

Durand moved to interpose himself between Desai and the alarm.

The geneticist held up his hands. "You do know whose lab this is, right?"

"Just listen." Durand approached Desai and pulled the LFP glasses off his face. "No phone calls, either."

Desai held up his hands. "Okay. Okay." He pointed to Durand's ID badge. "What happened to Marty?"

Durand pointed to a lab stool. "Sit down, and I'll go over it."

Desai looked around for some way to call help. "Look, I can pay. Whatever gang you're with, agreements can be struck. We're business-men, here."

"I'm not here to shake you down."

"How did you even know this lab was here and what to—"

"Just calm down."

Desai was starting to hyperventilate. "I support my entire extended family. Okay? I've got kids. Nephews, nieces. Aunts, uncles. Grandpar-ents. I—"

Desai swept a metal tray off the counter toward Durand—and then made a run for the opposite end of the lab.

Durand deflected the tray with his arm. Angry at the pain, he sprinted after Desai, his baseball cap flying off as he caught up to the fifty-year-old scientist with ease. Durand grabbed Desai by the collar and pulled him up sharply—shoving him back against the long lab counter and cabinets, rattling glass vials and beakers. "Would you calm down, goddamnit? I'm not here to hurt you. I'm here to ask for your help."

Desai's eyes went wide, and he suddenly looked more amazed than afraid. "Oh my god."

Durand looked up at his own reflection in the glass cabinet just behind Desai. His complement of tattoos was reappearing, arching across his scalp, neck, and hands. Apparently the sudden pain of getting hit with the metal tray had set it off. He looked menacing as hell—scowling with a bruised face and bloodshot eyes. He tried to soften his expression, but it was difficult.

Desai stared closely. "What is that?" He straightened and held up his hands in a gesture of reconciliation. "My apologies. Apologies. My god—they're getting darker." Desai laughed in spite of himself. "Those are amazing."

Durand released Desai, who immediately tried to touch Durand's face. Durand swatted his plump hands away. "Never mind the tattoos. I'm here for a different reason."

"But those are incredible. That synbio IP is worth more than this entire lab."

"I came here because you're an informant for Interpol."

Desai suddenly went back into panic mode again. "Whoa! I don't have any contact with Interpol, my friend. I swear to you. I am completely—"

Durand grabbed Desai by his lab coat lapels once more. "Would you shut up? I'm trying to tell you something."

Desai fell silent, but Durand could feel the man shaking.

"I'm not asking you whether you're an informant. I know you are."

"No, I promise."

Durand pounded the counter. "Shut up!"

Desai fell silent again.

He jabbed a thick finger into the man's face. "You are Radheya Desai, black market geneticist. You work for Pinjab, but you are a police informant."

Desai shook his head.

"Your handlers are Ling Ho and Martin Peele—aliases for agents with Interpol's Genetic Crime Division."

"No, no—"

"I know this because *I'm* the man you know as Martin Peele." Durand held up his ID badge, with the photo of Kenneth Durand on it, along with his alias name.

Desai glanced at the two different faces. "I don't understand."

Durand released his grip on the man's coat. "Neither do I. That's why I need your help."

"You look nothing like Martin Peele—if I even *knew* a Martin Peele. Which I do not."

"Rad, I instructed the Singapore police to raid this facility in March of last year. Since then, you've been passing me intelligence on chemical compounds, holding companies, and shipping addresses for embryo clinic suppliers."

Desai shook his head vigorously. "We don't edit human embryos here."

"I know you don't. But DNA is the same across all species. You use a lot of the same precursor materials as human embryo mills. Your usefulness to me is the only reason the SPF tolerates your existence."

Desai now looked grim-faced. "Okay, for the sake of argument, let's pretend that was true. What do you want from me . . . 'Mr. Peele'?"

Durand got right into Desai's face. "Someone edited my DNA. I think that someone was Marcus Wyckes—the leader of the Huli jing. You've heard of the Huli jing, right?"

Desai nodded.

"I need your help."

Durand was expecting more resistance, but instead Desai simply put a rubber-gloved hand to his mouth. "Wow . . ."

Durand observed Desai warily.

"The Huli jing edited your DNA."

Durand nodded.

"You do realize that's impossible—to edit a living, breathing organism. The changes would—"

"Yes. I know. The template wouldn't match. The organism would die before— I know all that. And yet apparently the Huli jing's bioengineers figured out a way."

Desai just stood shaking his head slowly. "I still—"

"Five weeks ago they injected me in the middle of a crowd of commuters. I woke up yesterday as a John Doe in an intensive care unit. Apparently the transformation happened while I was in a coma. They said I was all swelled up."

Desai considered this. He gestured toward Durand's tattoos. "And those?"

Durand examined his arm. "Whatever these are appeared at the same time. I don't even know why they come and go. They seem to be linked to my emotional state."

Desai motioned tentatively. "May I see your arm?"

"Sure." Durand warily extended his arm onto the counter as Desai grabbed a head-mounted magnifying glass from a nearby shelf.

"We'll go old-school since you've taken my LFPs . . ."

Desai peered closely at Durand's skin. The tattoos were beginning to fade right before their eyes. "Remarkable. This is remarkable work." He looked up. "May I put your arm under my microscope, Mr. Peele?"

Durand nodded.

"I will need my LFP glasses. They're linked to the device—but I assure you"—he held up his hand—"I will not misuse its connection. I simply want to confirm what I'm seeing."

Durand glowered but then passed the LFP glasses lying on the counter over to Desai. "I'm not in the mood for any tricks."

Desai put them on, and they both moved over to the sophisticated microscope.

Looking gleeful, Desai removed samples he already had in place and expanded the viewing area. He motioned, and Durand eased his hand into place beneath its lens. "Palm down on the counter, please. There. Be still." He examined the virtual imagery in his glasses. "What have we here . . . ?" He gasped. "My, my, my . . ." He looked up and smiled in genuine amazement.

"What do you see?"

"I did not think it possible. What year were you born?"

"Two thousand ten."

He waved it away. "Of course, of course, way too old to have received these edits in vitro. CRISPR didn't even exist then. Somehow you have specialized cells known as chromatophores seamlessly woven into your skin. My microscope just confirmed their structure."

"What are they?"

"You could think of them as *genetic tattoos*. They appear identical in structure to that of a chameleon—the topmost layer transparent with subsequent layers containing various pigments; xanthophores for yellow, erythrophores for red, cyanophores for blue, melanophores for brown— you get the idea. In a chameleon the colors are locked away in tiny vesicles so they don't normally appear. But they react to the central nervous system and are sensitive to chemicals in the bloodstream, making their colors visible when under duress or—"

"Excitement. Emotion."

"Precisely. Mood. Most people think the color changes of a chameleon are for camouflage, but they're actually to convey information to enemies and potential mates. Fascinating creatures, really."

Durand pulled his now normal-looking arm clear. "And you've seen this type of thing before?"

Desai lifted up his LFP glasses and rubbed his eyes. He shook his head. "No. And up until this moment, I didn't think such a thing was technologically possible." He turned to regard Durand. "You say that someone genetically edited you?"

"These tattoos are the least of it. They changed my ethnicity. My body. My face."

Desai examined Durand closely. "You mentioned your body swelled up—after receiving an injection?"

"I could barely breathe. Then I blacked out. The doctor said my skin got scabrous while I was in the coma."

Desai pondered this. "Like a chrysalis."

"I don't know. The hospital staff couldn't ID me. It's like my DNA got scrambled. I woke up to this . . ." Durand gestured at his reflection in a nearby glass cabinet.

Desai picked up the ID on Durand's lanyard and held the photo up alongside Durand's new face. "No obvious likeness. At all."

"My vocal cords. My hands. My body. Look, I know this sounds insane, but somehow the Huli jing figured out how to edit the living. Do you realize what this means for humanity?"

Desai seemed focused on his own thoughts. "I'd heard whispers in certain circles."

"What kind of whispers?"

"About in vivo edits."

"Hold it—you've *heard* of this?"

Desai nodded. "They say the increased processing power of photonic computing provided a window into epigenetics."

Durand didn't know whether to hug the man or punch him in the face. "Why the hell didn't you tell Interpol?"

Desai shrugged. "Because it was ridiculous. The type of thing one hears from synth addicts. From wishful-thinking trustafarian transhumanists."

"Back up. What did you hear, when, and from whom?"

"Whispered rumors of an elite black market where they edit the living."

"Who's 'they'?"

He nodded sheepishly. "The Huli jing . . . I'll grant you the rumor was about the Huli jing."

Durand pulled his phablet out and displayed the Interpol Red Notice on its screen. It displayed Durand's new DNA, photo, and listed his name as Marcus Wyckes.

"Apparently the Huli jing edited me to match the DNA profile of their leader, Marcus Wyckes. So now I'm wanted for all his crimes in one hundred and ninety countries. They turned me into the criminal I was hunting for."

Desai picked up the phablet, studying the Red Notice. "I saw the news. And here you are."

"I'm not this man, Rad. You have to believe me."

"Something tells me that if you were this man, I would already be dead. And the real Marcus Wyckes wouldn't need my help, in any case."

Durand looked at his reflection again in the cabinet glass. "I need to get back to who I was. Is that possible?"

Desai studied the photo on the front page of the Red Notice. Then he looked up. "Wait a minute. I think I know your real name. You're that Interpol agent who disappeared a month or so ago." He started searching the news. "It starts with a 'D.'"

Durand grabbed the phablet.

Desai held up his hands in peace. "You must forgive me, but your cover is, as they say in America, 'blown.' It is just a search away."

Durand sighed. "Durand. Kenneth Durand."

"Ah, Mr. Durand. Pleasure to finally meet you. And I might have good news for you."

"Let's hear it."

"The good news is that a GlobalFiler DNA profile consists of a minuscule percentage of a person's entire genomic sequence—just forty-six letters out of three billion. And that's all *noncoding* DNA—meaning it doesn't have any effect on physical appearance."

"Okay. So . . ."

"To make your DNA profile a preliminary match for Marcus Wyckes's, the Huli jing wouldn't need to change your physical appearance at all. They'd just have to change forty-six noncoding letters in all of your thirty-five trillion cells—a tall order, of course, but it's all relative."

"But they *did* change my appearance, and it's obvious why: to rob me of my identity and to make me a wanted man."

"Because?"

"Because I was a threat to them. I've been shutting down their labs."

Desai nodded. "And yet a complete transformation to this Wyckes fellow would not be necessary to frame you. They would likely restrict their edits to purely phenotypical traits—skin color, facial features, eye color, musculature—because changes to your organs would probably start to kill you."

"Meaning you don't think I'm *completely* changed."

"Right." He raised the Red Notice and pointed at the DNA ladders. "This minuscule GlobalFiler DNA profile would usually be sufficient to convict you. But I think a more complete sequencing would reveal that much of your original internals remain."

"How much of my DNA do you think the Huli jing edited?"

Desai studied Durand closely. "If I had access to some of your original DNA, I could tell for certain. But you must realize that all of humanity is 99.8 percent genetically identical. Just one-fifth of a percentage point is all that comprises our individual genetic identity."

"That little?"

Desai shrugged. "But we could compare your current genomic sequence to that of the real Marcus Wyckes—assuming the authorities have his original DNA."

"They do."

"I'm guessing there'll be a difference. That should prove to the authorities that you aren't Wyckes. But to prove your identity as Kenneth Durand we'd need a sample of your original DNA."

Durand produced the plastic bag containing his original hair. "I lifted it from my flat just before I came here."

"Marvelous." Desai held the bag up to the light. "It'll take a few hours to sequence. I'll need to draw blood from you as you are now—we can run the sequencing in parallel. Afterward, assuming I'm correct, I could approach the authorities with the evidence—perhaps your partner, Mr. Ling?"

Durand took a moment to consider his options. After several seconds he shook his head. "No."

Desai looked surprised. "No?"

"We're not doing that."

"I thought you wanted to get your identity back."

"It's not just my identity I want back. I want my physical form back. My own DNA."

Desai put a hand to his chin. "Well, if this sort of change is occurring somewhere in the world, then the technology will eventually—"

"You don't seem to understand the full implications of live editing."

Desai laughed ruefully. "Oh, I do. I realize how much this innovation is worth, certainly."

"Think beyond that. The ability to edit living people undermines the very foundation of authority—namely the ability to *uniquely* identify human beings. If DNA can be edited in living people, there's no way to hold anyone accountable anymore. For *anything*. This procedure will be *far* more illegal than embryo edits ever were—by a long shot."

Desai contemplated this.

"I know the law. They won't make an exception for me, Rad. They might promise to help me, but they'll never do it. I'll be a casualty in the war on genetic edits. They'll tell me to just accept it."

Desai said nothing.

"How can I make love to my wife as Marcus Wyckes? Or have my six-year-old daughter accept me? I *must* get back to the way I was. I need to get this man's DNA out of me. Do you understand?"

Desai proceeded cautiously. "Is it the Asian aspect that—?"

He pounded the counter again. "My wife and child are Asian, you idiot. I'm not a racist—I just want my self back."

"I see." Desai spread his hands. "I'm sorry, but I don't see how that's possible, Mr. Durand."

"The Huli jing already showed it's possible. They edited me once. It must be possible to be edited again."

Desai paced his lab. "Look. To be entirely honest, I'm not an actual geneticist. Not really."

Durand narrowed his eyes at the man.

"I'm more of a glorified technician. I tell people I'm a geneticist because—"

Durand felt himself getting mad. His tattoos began to reappear.

Desai held up his hands. "What you need to do is talk to a full-fledged *genetic engineer*. Fortunately, I know an excellent one. He could tell you whether it's possible to get changed back."

"Who is he?"

"A man who can be trusted."

"How do you know he won't turn me in?"

"Because, like you, he's a wanted man. One problem, though: he's not in Singapore."

"Can we get him on an AR conference line?"

Desai winced. "He avoids phones."

"Can you get him to come here?"

"Mmm . . . that's the thing. Singapore is one of the countries where he's wanted." Desai clapped. "Fortunately, though, he's just across the Strait in Johor Bahru."

"You expect me to cross the border into Malaysia? How the hell can I get across the Strait? Every cop in Singapore is expecting me to cross the border."

Desai patted Durand's shoulder. "Not to worry. We cross the border all the time."

Chapter 17

Radheya Desai and Kenneth Durand arrived via a freight elevator at a subbasement of the Agriville farm tower. They then moved through several locked doors, and finally through a hidden panel disguised as a plain cement wall.

They entered a large concrete chamber with an open pool of water in the center. The space was lined with metal shelving packed to overflowing with fiber-optic and electroactive polymer extruders, photonics boards, and rebreather gear. Likewise, an entire aquarium of lifelike robotic fish hung on racks or splayed across shelves. It was like a robotic theme park storage room.

"What's all this?" Durand sifted through the shelves as two Hoklo workers entered from a doorway on the far side of the room.

Desai barked at the men in Hokkien. Then he turned to Durand. "Underwater air lock. Leads right into the Strait of Johor. We use this to smuggle biotech wares out of Singapore via autonomous subs."

Durand felt the rubbery fin of an artificial marlin. "Robotic fish?"

"Electroactive polymers. Soft robotics." Desai shrugged. "The SPF and Malaysian officials have lots of drones searching for other drones. But *fish*—especially endangered species—get a free pass. Except with poachers, of course, but our fish are not likely to wander into purse seine nets because they monitor fishing trawler radar signals—and avoid them. Something real fish do not do."

Durand studied the shelves and wall pegs overflowing with robotic fish. "How does this get me to Johor?"

"Ah . . ."

Durand turned to see that the two Chinese workers had left, and now he heard the scraping rattle of metal as they pushed open twin rusting metal doors to a neighboring room—revealing a life-sized replica of a great white shark. It was at least twenty feet long and suspended in a harness, secured by chains to a rusting overhead rail system that squealed as the men pushed the artificial shark along the track.

"You have got to be shitting me."

"No! We've only rarely used it. Most of our shipments are deliberately small. However, 'Bruce' here sometimes comes in handy." Desai motioned for the men to bring the soft robotic shark all the way into the room and alongside the opening to the pool of water.

"You're yanking my chain."

"No, indeed."

"You've sent a human being in that thing across the Strait of Johor?"

Desai hesitated. "Not a *living* person, no. But at least we know you'll fit." He clapped Durand on the back. "We'll set Bruce to a neutral buoyancy for your weight." He escorted Durand onto a scale.

Durand was fifteen kilos heavier than he'd ever been. Given his build, it certainly wasn't fat.

"You're a bit heavier than our last passenger, and neither did he need breathing apparatus. But I'm sure we can get it to work."

One of the Chinese workers opened a locker and pulled out rebreather equipment.

"You know how to use a rebreather?"

"Yes. I learned in the navy." Durand eyed the robotic shark skeptically. "How do I know you're not just trying to kill me?"

"There are cheaper ways to kill you. But you must also realize that I have more than a passing interest in whether this in vivo editing of yours is real. I'm every bit as eager as you are to learn more. And my friend will be able to tell us both a great deal."

Durand felt irritation at Desai's implication, but he decided not to say anything. Instead, he stared at the robotic shark as one of the workers tapped at an old, ruggedized computer tablet—causing the shark's mouth to open wide.

Durand could see all the way down its gullet.

Desai turned to him with a smile. "It can accept a payload of a hundred and fifty kilos. And we haven't lost it yet."

Durand looked into the creature's mouth and tested its rows of teeth with his finger. They flexed. *Rubber.*

Desai leaned in next to him and winced at the odor coming out of the depths. "Wang, you should have kept it stored with its mouth open, lah. It never dried out from last time. There are puddles inside."

They began to argue in Hokkien.

Durand studied the interior. "You disposed of a body with this. Who and why?"

"A Yakuza—mortally wounded in a gun battle with Singapore police. His family wanted him back in Japan for burial. We helped spirit his remains out of the country, so to speak."

"All the way to *Japan*?"

Desai laughed. "Of course not. Just across the Strait. It's just a few kilometers. Liquid metal batteries give this a range of approximately sixteen kilometers, so you'll have plenty of power. We have a matching underwater airlock in Johor. You'll be able to get past all the underwater scanners, border control drones. You name it."

Durand again leaned into the shark's mouth. The reek was revolting—a mix of rotten fish, dirty socks, and ozone. He could see a pallet-like platform six feet long and two feet wide, with straps for securing a load. It was perhaps a foot high. It was going to be tight indeed—especially with his new body. "I lie down on that?"

Desai nodded. "Have any fear of closed spaces?"

"No."

"You will." He then reached in and pulled out the platform like a drawer—although it more accurately resembled a shark's tongue depressor.

One of the workers behind him held up the rebreather gear and spoke with a thick Hokkien accent. "Ready, lah?"

It took about fifteen minutes for Durand to get suited up. He then lay on his stomach on the pallet platform as Desai went back over the procedure yet again. Durand was filled with anxiety; lying in the mouth of a great white shark brought to mind the end of some classic movie.

Desai patted Durand's shoulder. "Don't worry. The shark will take care of everything. It will evade boats and drones on its own. It's programmed to know where to go. We think we've got the buoyancy calculations right, so you shouldn't sink to the ocean floor."

"You *think* you've got them right?"

"It's math. You trust math, right?"

"It's not math I'm worried about."

"You'll travel at a depth of ten meters—roughly two atmospheres of pressure. So decompression won't be a problem. That is, unless some major evasive action is necessary—in which case you might need some decompression time. But not to worry! We'll sort all that out if necessary. There's a VR display in your face mask that's hooked into cameras in the front and sides of the machine—so you can get a solid visual of the swim."

"How long?"

"Twenty minutes—give or take depending on tides, currents, and evasion of authorities, smugglers, poachers, and fishing nets."

"The little details."

"I'll be honest with you: this will not be pleasant. I want to be clear on that. But given how wanted you are by the police, it's the only way to smuggle you across the border."

Durand reluctantly nodded.

"I'll meet you on the other side."

With that, Desai slapped Durand on the shoulder one more time and put his full-face rebreather mask on, which Durand began to adjust. Desai made a circular motion with his hand to the Chinese workers.

Durand felt the pallet platform move slowly into the gullet of the shark—and the rubbery electroactive polymer material suddenly squeezed in on him from all sides. He felt a growing panic of confinement. It was like climbing into a rubber coffin. Massive electroactive polymer muscles constricted on him as the machine went through its diagnostics.

And then the mouth of the shark closed. Complete blackness.

Durand heard whirring winch motors and felt the shark swaying back and forth. A moment later a video image projected into his retinas—and light streamed in. He could see a wide-angle view forward and to the sides of the shark's head.

Desai stood near the air lock, next to a worker holding the winch controls. He smiled and gave a thumbs-up sign.

Durand could hear only his heart pounding in his ears. Air had started flowing from the rebreather, but he still felt like he was suffocating.

And then the bottom dropped out.

From the video he could tell that someone had detached the harness and let the synthetic shark drop into the pool of water. Durand nearly panicked as the artificial musculature of the robotic fish launched into action, noiselessly squeezing him like a vise as it twisted right, then left.

And then cold water poured in all around him.

He tried to disregard the feeling of drowning, but being unable to draw breath every time the shark's muscles clenched didn't help.

But he was locked in place. He couldn't move.

He opened his eyes to see in the video feed that his artificial shark was sweeping forward through a tubelike concrete tunnel. Up ahead, he could see a steel gate opening slowly with a grinding sound. There were barnacles and smaller fish all around—some of which fled at the looming terror of this six-meter fish.

With each sweep of its tail, the artificial muscles squeezed the air out of Durand, causing him to cough as he sucked for oxygen—and then get a mouthful of salt water through the distorted rubber seals. Then the shark's musculature would relax, and Durand would gulp air before the cycle began again.

The shark plunged downward now. Durand tried to take in the underwater scene, but constriction crushed him.

It was an advanced design, he did not doubt—no moving parts, just electroactive polymers contracting like muscle tissue under the guidance of a computer brain—but it was clear this machine wasn't designed for a living passenger.

The shark leveled out and began swimming across the murky, sandy seabed. The depth gauge in the corner of his video feed indicated that he was at ten meters depth almost exactly. But the seabed was dropping out beneath him.

And yet everything seemed under control. Durand tried to calm his rising sense of claustrophobia. He looked down and could see the trash-strewn seabed of the Strait of Johor. There was the rusted shell of a car. A sunken fishing boat. Various steel barrels and barnacle-encrusted billboards.

Not as many fish as he'd expected, though. Lots of jellyfish—some of them huge. The artificial shark didn't seem to notice any but the largest of these. They were vast translucent organisms, some of them tens of meters long. They caught the sunlight from above as they floated, their gossamer-like stingers trailing. Durand had to admit they were beautiful, but he knew why they were proliferating. He'd read about acidification of the oceans—how the rising acidity harmed fish and the formation of shells, fostering what was called "jellification" of the seas; jellyfish thrived in the new environment, whereas more advanced life-forms—like fish—did not.

Ahead he could see an endless field of jellyfish, dotting the depths like eerie spaceships.

And then Durand saw something else—a torpedo-like craft surging along in front of a whirring screw. Even deep within the belly of the artificial shark, he could hear the shrill piercing of its sensors scanning as it passed below them, from left to right, heading along the coast. A black torpedo with the logo of the Singapore Customs department on its flank.

The shark leaned to the left, and then dove down in a move that put Durand's stomach in his throat. He resisted the urge to vomit—which he knew would probably cause him to suffocate. He couldn't even raise his hand to his face. His robotic monster swam deeper and Durand could feel the pressure in his ears. But they moved clear of the customs drone.

As he looked downward now, Durand saw they were much closer to the seabed, moving between piles of garbage and rocks. Here, too, he could see lidar, radar, and heat sensors of all types—hear their ear-drilling sonar beeps and frequency scanning. The place was a solid wall of underwater sensors.

The anti-terror security measures were for good reason. Not everyone in the world was pleased about Singapore's success, and not everyone wished it well.

The shark undulated forward, sweeping its tail tirelessly as it headed off a cliff and out across the much deeper channel. A murky abyss yawed below—not more than sixty meters deep, he knew, but due to the low visibility it might as well have been a thousand.

Then the hiss of a ship's propeller and the drone of a big engine rose above all the other sounds. Durand turned right and left to see where it was coming from. It seemed almost upon them, but then it kept getting louder. Something truly huge was headed his way.

When it had become almost deafening, he finally saw ahead a black wall moving into his view from the left—with a range of numbers printed on it that, having been in the navy, he knew well. They were depth measurements, in meters. The numbers went to fifteen—and that's when he realized it was a monstrous container ship, with a draft in excess of forty-five feet.

It was sliding in front of them at a distance of a hundred meters, a rolling wall of steel—followed, he well knew, by three or more propellers five meters in diameter, moving fast enough to kill with cavitations alone anything that came close to them.

Durand turned his eyes as far left as they could go to see the approaching propellers—horrified that the shark wasn't yet diving deep. It needed to dive! He struggled with rising panic, but could still not move. The damn shark was heading right toward the wall of the ship, and if it only dove just beneath it, the propellers might roll in right on top of them—cutting them to ribbons.

Durand felt panic and started hyperventilating—but then the shark dove, and he mentally urged it to continue diving as the water pressure closed in on him, making it still harder to catch his breath between vise-like constrictions of the shark's musculature.

And then Durand saw the whirling cavitation patterns of the quad screws rolling in above them—and not nearly far enough away.

The impact of their pressure wave crushed the top of the shark down into him, squeezing every ounce of breath from Durand's body as the shark was swept aside like a bathtub toy. He heard straining metamaterials creaking all around him as the shark continued to struggle, and finally rolled over.

The video feed went black.

The entire machine simply stopped functioning. Limp, it began to sink, still buffeted by the deafening roar of the propeller wash above.

No!

Durand strained against the impenetrable skin of the robotic monster and cursed himself for not asking for a diving knife. He might have been able to cut himself free. Instead, he watched in horror as the video feed stayed black. The shark kept rolling, rolling. The water pressure increased. Then the shark thumped onto the seabed.

His ears felt the crushing depth, and he knew he was finished. It was all quiet now, with the ship's roar receding fast, but the shark was still in utter darkness.

And then he heard beeping and felt constrictions in several of the shark's muscle groups. It was a pattern that a computerphile instinctively knew.

A reboot.

A terminal cursor appeared in his vision, and then computer scripts rushed past.

The shark had crashed. That must have been it. Maybe it didn't like the readings it was getting. Maybe something got a voltage spike. Whatever it was, the great artificial shark started to come back to life, and with relief Durand felt its crushing wave of muscle contractions come over him again. Squeezing the air out of him once more.

He was never so happy to feel partially suffocated.

Nearly an hour later—about three times longer than he'd expected—the synthetic shark ceased its slow, upward decompression spirals and finally entered the mouth of the Sungai Kim inlet across the border in Malaysia. He could see a couple of customs sensors on the ocean floor, but nothing compared with the great array monitoring Singapore.

Before long the false shark was swinging its tail against a current and into a smuggler's cove. Durand heard the whining screws of smaller boats, but after his experience with the monstrous container ship, he wasn't nearly as concerned. Instead, he was struggling with real suffocation. His rebreather mouthpiece had become partly dislodged from the air hose during one of the shark's muscle contractions—and now every time he had to draw air, he barely got enough. He felt himself near to hypoxia and knew that if he passed out he'd die—since he wouldn't be able to time or maximize his breaths to the shark's movements.

Durand closely watched his progress into the cove on the video monitor as the shark moved into shallower and shallower water—finally reaching a depth of barely ten meters. He could see pier piles ahead, and the shark moved directly into their barnacle-encrusted forest-like depths.

And then suddenly the shark surged upward, finally relaxing its muscles as Durand heard a hissing sound—actuators releasing compressed air.

In a few moments, the video feed revealed that he'd surfaced in another air lock, one not dissimilar to the air lock he'd left in Singapore. He realized that identical portals would suit a robotic shark. Robots liked predictable apertures. The shark bobbed in the sloshing waves of the small opening.

Durand felt the shark get winched out of the water, and finally watched as workers with hard hats motioned for others to lower the shark onto a concrete floor.

Only then did the shark's mouth open, and Durand immediately used the freedom of movement to pull the rebreather mask off his face. He sucked for air as fast as he could, coughing out seawater.

After his breathing calmed, he looked up to see Desai, now wearing a fedora, suit, and tie, and clutching a gold-handled cane.

Desai smiled. "Your tattoos communicate that you are upset with me. But in my defense, if I had been honest about how unpleasant that journey would be, you might not have done it. And now look: you are in Johor Bahru, my friend."

Durand resisted the urge to punch Desai's smiling face.

Malaysian workers activated the platform inside the shark, causing

Durand to emerge from the shark's mouth as though it were regurgitating a surfboard.

As soon as he was free, Durand shakily got to his feet. Desai helped hold him upright. Durand took a deep breath as he looked around. No police or armed men about. Desai had apparently not betrayed him.

Durand finally nodded. "You're right. I wouldn't have gotten in there if I knew what was coming."

Desai slapped him on the back. "That's the spirit! Now come on. Let's get you out of those wet clothes. We have someone to see."

An hour later Durand and Desai exited an electric van driven by one of Desai's confederates. Durand wore a wide-brimmed bush hat, baggy cargo shorts, a plain button-down shirt, and sandals. He gazed at the cityscape around him.

Durand had been to Johor Bahru several times. As far as he was concerned, it was a cheap shopping destination for Singaporeans—ringed with shopping malls, restaurants, low-cost entertainments. The last time he'd been here was to buy furniture for Mia's bedroom.

But he'd never wandered into the industrial backstreets—which was where they were now. He could see the additive printing houses, bio-manufacturing plants, and photonic part suppliers that no one had ever heard of. Hundreds of migrant workers moved around him interacting with invisible AR objects and speaking to invisible people back home. He heard a smattering of Bengali, Indonesian, Vietnamese, and Burmese. It was a pale imitation of Singapore's synbio industry—but the spillover was still substantial.

Desai led him down a narrow lane of smaller shops and teeming apartment blocks. They passed a row of laser vision-correction vending machines. Real-world signage was on display all around him, but also rogue light field projectors, creating ghostly "adparitions" of Asian models hawking beer and energy drinks, with captions in various languages scrolling in midair.

Desai pushed a pair of mirror glasses into Durand's hand. "The ad mix gets aggressive here in Johor."

Durand slipped on the mirror glasses and half the advertising disappeared. But one sign close at hand did not. It cast a glow over them both in the fading light of the humid evening. It was an old-fashioned, real-life neon sign buzzing the word "Twisted" into life letter by letter, with a double helix of DNA serving as a swizzle stick in a martini glass.

Durand cast a doubtful look at Desai.

"Never heard of it?"

"No. And if it mattered, I would have."

Desai laughed. "Embryo labs aren't the only things of interest in this world, Mr. Durand."

Durand followed Desai down a dark flight of stone steps.

They entered through an ancient wooden door into a dimly lit vestibule—and were immediately deafened by cacophonous guitar and synthesis sounds. Durand winced at the random musical gibberish.

Desai motioned and pulled Durand farther inside. After a few moments they passed through a sonic wall and immediately found themselves in comparative silence. They moved through a velvet curtain into a darkened, ornate bar buzzing with conversation and soft ambient music.

"Apologies for the sonic assault at the entrance. Protein music discourages casual tourists. That sounded like tomato DNA actually . . ."

Durand removed his mirror glasses and surveyed the place—an eighteenth-century Asian watering hole, with curtained booths and a crowded British-colonial-period bar, beveled mirrors and carved teak wood. In an earlier century it might have been an opium den. Original gas lamps barely illuminated the room—and its unusual clientele. Strangely attired patrons with anti-facial-recognition paint in stylish Día de los Muertos patterns, electronic tattoos of Chinese characters or animated cartoon characters glittering across bald scalps, motorized piercings (earlobe-mounted gear mechanisms seemed popular), ornate cosmetic surgical stitches, and other enhancements from devil horns to fangs filled the room.

"And they said bio-punk was dead."

"Don't mock what you don't understand."

Durand's gaze moved from person to person. They spanned all ages and races; male, female, and transgender. "Biohackers."

"I'm told they prefer the term *extra-humanists*."

"These aren't geneditors, Rad. They're tweakers. Surgical and chemical modification isn't going to help me. What are we doing here?"

"Patience." Desai led him farther into the establishment, squeezing past the crowd at the bar. Durand edged past a buxom Caucasian woman in a corset and a Victorian hat—her skin glowed softly in the semidarkness as if she were a ghost. Durand shielded his eyes to see if she was an AR projection, but she remained.

Desai whispered, "Bioluminescent elixirs—popular with party people. Wears off after a few hours. Many's the office worker whose midnight proclivities are revealed when they arrive, still glowing, to the office the next morning."

The woman's gaze followed Durand with obvious interest. It shocked him how unabashed she was, and what was stranger was how magnetic he felt. Confident as he strode through the crowd, which was something he'd never felt in crowds before.

They moved through another sonic compartment of the open room, where the ambient music was replaced by thumping dance music and lights.

Desai leaned back to speak as he continued to move through the dancers. "They augment themselves, you see. Imbibe chemicals, endure radical surgeries. All to extend their natural senses, abilities, and appearance—some of it only temporary. But all in an effort to make their physical form match the person they see in their mind's eye."

Durand watched as he passed a booth where black-eyed young men speaking in Russian watched one of their number inject a companion in the eyeball. The liquid turned the man's eye completely black in seconds.

"Ocular reagent—gives a limited ability to see invisible spectrums of light. Ultraviolet. Temporary, of course. The body metabolizes it."

"And just think, all you have to do is inject yourself in the eye."

"The world has all types. I think it's marvelous." Desai brought them onward.

"How's this place stay open? I thought Malaysia was a conservative country."

"Malaysia has its own method of dealing with human nature. Almost nothing is allowed. But that's what fines are for. None of this would be tolerated in Singapore, of course, but many of these people work for the biggest synbio firms in Singapore. 'Straities,' they're called. There is money in this room, my friend."

Durand pushed past a young man with artificial horns protruding from his skull. Durand nodded to him as he edged by.

Another man sitting in a booth wore a thin film display on his chest, revealing an ultrasound image of his heart beating and trachea swallowing as he downed his drink.

Desai pointed. "Chip implanters, body modders, quantified-self addicts. You'll find all types here. Perhaps some of them have edited somatic cells—blood, sperm, and so on. But nothing as ambitious as what you've experienced."

The vibe was clearly more relaxed than in Singapore. Durand had been aware of this at some level but had never seen it firsthand—and he found it fascinating. More than a few women—and also a few men—cast looks his way. He strode through and others made way for him. He was intimidating, and with shame he felt elated by it.

Desai led Durand toward a roped entrance to a back room, guarded by a burly Chinese bouncer in a pin-striped suit and black derby that Durand guessed was loaded with sensor gear. Maybe even nonlethal weaponry. The huge man stared at Desai for a moment—getting a face-rec match apparently. His expression suddenly softened, no doubt after the CRM system told him to smile courteously and unhinge a velvet rope. "Mr. Desai. Good evening, sir."

Desai motioned. "This young man is with me, Ferar."

"Very good, sir. Will you be—"

"No, we'll be joining Dr. Frey this evening."

"Very good, sir."

Durand squeezed past the bouncer, avoiding the man's stare lest management get a face-rec match on him as well.

Desai led the way down an aisle of Persian carpet, bordered by closed velvet curtains and richly carved mahogany dragons. They caught glimpses of smiling faces, the sharp scent of atomized narcotics, and laughter through narrow openings. Then Desai stopped and knocked with his cane on a wooden dragon head—the number "13" clutched in its fanged mouth.

A man's voice called from within. "What sort of idiot knocks on a curtain?"

Desai nodded to Durand and pushed through.

Durand followed.

Inside, instead of the private booth he had expected, there was a small sitting room, with normal-sized chairs arrayed around a shorter-than-usual table, at which sat a dwarf with a brooding, handsome face and tousled brown hair. He wore a collared silk shirt and LFP glasses adapted to fit antique frames. The room was otherwise covered in Persian carpets, velvet throw pillows with tassels, and oil paintings of twentieth-century Asian businessmen in suits and ties. It was as though someone had furnished the place entirely from the bankruptcy auctions of pre–fourth industrial revolution companies and raided bordellos.

Durand guessed the dwarf was under a meter and a half tall. Except for his diminutive arms and legs, he was normally proportioned and clattered away on a totem keyboard. Several other inscrutable totem devices stood on the table beside him. Durand knew those inert pieces of plastic would look quite different through LFP glasses.

A piece of crystal stemware also stood on the table, its mouth bridged by an ornate silver spoon holding a sugar cube. An open bottle of absinthe stood close by along with a pitcher of water. Vapor wafted upward from the man's 1930s-style vape pen. A blister pak of printed pharmaceuticals also sat open on the table, with two tabs out of four empty.

Desai and Durand eased into rattan chairs on the far side of the table. The dwarf's unwelcoming stare followed them both.

He took a pull from his vape pen and spoke with a mid-Atlantic American accent as vapor curled around him. "Radheya Desai. Not a face I've seen in a while. I heard you were farming juice boxes back in the Bubble."

"We all have bills to pay."

"I see you brought a menacing stranger along." He resumed tapping at his totem keyboard. "Unannounced."

Desai smiled. "A business opportunity, Bryan."

Durand cast a wary look Desai's way.

"Dr. Bryan Frey, please meet . . ." Desai gestured to Durand. "Let's just say a most fascinating friend."

Frey continued typing. "I have yet to meet any friend of yours I'd call fascinating."

"Then this will be the exception." Desai turned to Durand. "Dr. Frey holds a degree in genetic engineering from the University of Bonn. His specialty is bioinformatics—computer modeling to develop new CRISPR edits for numerous species."

Durand watched Frey still tapping away. "Human edits?"

Frey spoke without looking up. "No, those would be *very* illegal. What I do is considerably less so."

Desai gestured. "He is an editor for hire—jail-breaking closed-loop proprietary agricultural sequences. He also creates edits for house pets and the occasional chemical biohack for humans—synthesized supplements, things of that sort."

"Anything that hardens dicks is a big seller." Frey glanced up. "In the humans, not the pets."

Durand eyed Frey dubiously.

"Look at it this way: I'm saving the rhinos."

Durand spoke to Desai. "You brought me to a back-alley gene hacker?"

Frey pointed to the door. "Piss off, 'most fascinating friend.'"

Desai motioned for calm. "Dr. Frey has an open mind, and he is an engineer of considerable talent."

Durand nodded to the printed pharmaceutical blister pak. "Yeah, he looks real solid. I crossed the Johor Strait to meet this guy?"

"I can think of no one better suited to answer your question."

Frey studied Durand. "Crossed over from Singapore, eh? The Orange County of Asia. Personally, I prefer my corruption a shade less self-righteous."

Desai turned to Frey. "A sonic curtain, if you please, Bryan."

Frey sighed. "Your mistake, Rad, is that you think anyone gives a shit about what you have to say." He fished in a nearby leather satchel and produced a metallic wand. With a click, three legs extended from it, and he placed it on the table. "This is a two-person unit, so we'll have to get chummy." He pressed a button. A high-pitched noise raced past them.

Durand was familiar with the devices—white noise projector. They generated a wall of scrambled audio—canceling vibrations within a sphere and generating random noise in its place. They'd be able to speak freely without being overheard by nearby microphones or eavesdroppers. Interpol's GCI was surrounded by them. The sonic walls near the bar doorway and the dance floor were based on similar principles.

As Durand pulled his chair close to the table, he and Desai passed through a field of noise that buzzed in their ears. Then the sound of the bar beyond vanished. The echoes now made it sound like they were conversing in a closet.

Desai leveled a stare at Frey. "Bryan, my friend here is wanted by the authorities."

Frey glowered. "You'd better mean *Singapore* authorities."

"Yes . . . among many others. And yet he is, himself, an Interpol agent."

Frey's face turned decidedly grim.

Desai continued. "He is, in fact, the lead analyst for Interpol's Genetic Crime Division. Possibly the man most responsible for the raids shutting down illicit embryo clinics worldwide." Desai gestured. "Dr. Bryan Frey, meet Agent Kenneth Durand."

Frey turned from one to the other man several times. "You brought an Interpol agent *here*—to my office? Are you insane?"

Desai motioned for calm. "There are reasons, Bryan."

"Reasons. I can't imagine any reason why you would bring a *world policeman* to see *me*—much less into this establishment." He gestured to the curtains. "Please leave, gentlemen. It is my sincere hope you do not get murdered on the way out. Although I wouldn't count on it."

Desai persisted. "This is a special case, Bryan. Look . . ." And with that Desai hauled off and slapped Durand across the face—the hit echoing in the closed acoustic environment.

The surprise of the slap was worse than its sting. Durand leaped up, grabbing Desai's wrist in a crushing hold. The table shook, toppling the bottle and pitcher.

Frey stood. "Careful, goddamnit!" He grabbed for the water pitcher. Durand used Desai's tie to pull him close. "What the hell, Rad?"

Desai winced as Durand's powerful fist held him. "Look, Bryan! Look." Desai pointed to Durand's face and neck.

Sure enough, Durand could see the tattoos fading into place on his forearms and the back of his hand as he held Desai in a crushing grip. No doubt they were doing the same on his neck and elsewhere.

Frey righted the spilled bottle, and looking up, his face went slack. He focused with new interest on Durand.

Durand released Desai. "You goddamned idiot."

Desai straightened his tie. "My apologies, Mr. Durand. But a picture is worth a thousand words, as they say."

Frey stared closely at Durand's arms as he wiped liquid off his inert keyboard. "I must confess I'm curious. What am I looking at?"

"Chromatophores, Bryan. Genetic tattoos. Integrated into his skin."

Frey gave an incredulous look. "No . . ."

"I have microscope slides. It's seamlessly integrated into his nervous system."

"How in the hell . . . ?"

Desai looked giddy. "Isn't it incredible?"

"Well, it might be incredible, but I'm curious why a 'wanted' Interpol agent is fronting exotic synbio. Are you offering the IP for sale, Mr. Durand?"

"The tattoos aren't why I'm here."

"Undercover—is that it? Thus the whole 'wanted man' nonsense?" Frey dropped the keyboard onto the table. "If you came here to recruit me as an informer—"

"Bryan, listen: these tattoos are nothing. *Nothing.* Mr. Durand is here to request your help on something much bigger."

Frey laughed ruefully. "Well, you can go screw yourself, Agent Durand—or whoever you are. You may have some impressive Straitie toys, but I don't talk to cops and no doubt the gentleman out front has already pegged you for a cop."

"I'm not here for Interpol. I came to ask for your help."

"Well, I don't want to help you." Frey jabbed his vape pen at Durand.

"World-government types like you are the reason I wasn't born both handsome *and* tall. My achondroplasia could have been corrected in vitro by my mother. A fairly straightforward mutation in the fibroblast growth factor receptor three gene that could have easily been modified. But no, because it wasn't on the 'UN-approved' list of genetic edits, I get to stare at people's crotches my whole life. Asshole."

Durand felt his temper flaring.

"The tattoos are intensifying, Bryan. See how they're linked to his central nervous system?"

"That is pretty impressive—"

Durand leaned across the table—almost up to Frey's face. "Listen, you shit. You have no idea what I went through to get here—"

"I pay rent here. If you so much as touch me, they'll find your body in the—"

Desai tugged at both the men's sleeves. "Please! Please. Gentlemen. Sit, Mr. Durand." Desai turned to Frey. "None of this matters. Bryan. Look at Mr. Durand—whom does he resemble?"

Frey glowered. *"Homo neanderthalensis?"*

"No! If you check the news, you will see that an Interpol agent named Kenneth Durand went missing over a month ago—presumably kidnapped by the Huli jing. Today Mr. Durand sits before you, physically transformed."

Frey glared. "I'm not in the mood for cryptic games, Rad. I'm busy. Now leave, both of you, before I have management throw you out."

"Mr. Durand was genetically edited, Bryan. The Huli jing edited him in vivo. *In vivo.* A mass genedit to a living organism. To a *living* adult human being."

Frey stopped cold. He looked intensely at Durand—then back at Desai. "Get the hell out of here."

"You've heard the rumors, same as me."

"People say lots of crazy shit, Rad. It's just talk."

"Is it?" Desai put his hand on Durand's muscular shoulder. "The Huli jing modified Mr. Durand's DNA, making him both a forensic profile match and phenotypical match for Marcus Wyckes. Look . . ."

Durand removed the phablet from his cargo pocket. The Interpol

Red Notice was still displayed on its screen as he slid it across the table to Frey.

"But I don't think it was a complete transformation—I think his vital organs remain unchanged. If we run a genetic sequence on this man and compare it to his original DNA, there will be massive overlap. You don't have to believe me; run bioinformatic models on both samples and the similarities should be obvious."

Frey watched Durand closely, and then snatched up the phablet, his eyes scanning the printed DNA ladders and the mug shot photo.

Desai pressed. "Search the newsfeeds. You will see photographs confirming that the man sitting before you is the infamous Marcus Wyckes—and yet he is not. Ask yourself: Why would Marcus Wyckes come to you for help? Marcus Wyckes has an army of bioengineers."

Frey scrolled down, quickly reading through. He finally looked up again. "Yes. I've heard rumors about living edits, but around here everyone wants to be something or someone else. Desperation makes them willing to believe any rumor." He slid the phablet back to Durand, eyeing his guest closely.

Durand stared back.

Frey then picked up his phone totem.

Durand's hand shot out to grab Frey's wrist. "You're not calling anyone."

Frey looked with impatience at the massive hand clutching his wrist. "I'm checking newsfeeds to confirm a few things. I'm sure a world policeman like yourself can appreciate the need to gather evidence."

Durand released Frey's arm.

"Keep your sausage fingers off me." Frey became engrossed in his virtual screens. He looked into space with the dreamlike trance of someone engaging with a private light field projection. He slid something unseen in line with Durand, apparently comparing reality to the virtual. "Well. There you are. Marcus Demang Wyckes. A twenty-first-century Pablo Escobar. Mass murderer. Slaver."

Frey lowered his arms, clearly engaging with the reality in front of him now. "I'd like to apologize if I have in any way—"

"Bryan! He's not Marcus Wyckes. I'm telling you."

Frey pondered the situation. "Well . . . there seems to be a reward of ten million yuan for his capture, dead or alive—though I don't imagine there will be many takers."

"The reward is nothing—*nothing*—compared to this technology, Bryan!"

Durand leaned forward. "I'm not Marcus Wyckes. I'm Kenneth Durand. The Huli jing hit me with some sort of injection that put me into a coma. I woke up like this, and I need to get changed back to my original DNA. What I need to know is whether that's possible. You're a genetic engineer. I need some answers."

Frey let out an exasperated laugh. "I'd be guessing."

"The Huli jing edited me once. Could they use my original DNA to change me back?"

Frey pondered the question. "You claim that you—an adult human—have been genetically edited, even though it's never been proven possible. My immediate reaction is that you're a raving lunatic."

Desai interjected, "You can sequence his DNA—"

Frey held up a silencing hand. "*Except.* Except your face is also undeniably all over the feeds as Marcus Wyckes and you've got some incredible synbio tech woven into your skin. Which means you're no run-of-the-mill lunatic." He sighed. "If you're really this Kenneth Durand—I would give anything to know what biotech was in that injection. It would have to be virally based—possibly XNA machinery—to get around the immune response."

Desai interjected. "He was swollen up like a balloon, Bryan."

"Like a chrysalis . . ."

"Yes, I thought the same thing!"

"Interesting . . ."

Durand ignored their apparent excitement. "Just answer my question. Could the Huli jing change me back to myself?"

Frey took a big pull on his vape pen. "If—and this is a big if—if Huli jing genetic engineers have developed the ability to edit *living organisms*. If they have somehow decoded gene expression, figured out how to evade all the body's natural defenses and rewrite genetic code even as you lived and all without instigating a necrotic cascade. If they can do that . . ."

Durand hung on Frey's words.

"I see no scientific reason why they couldn't reverse it."

Durand slumped in relief.

Desai leaned in. "Think about it, Bryan: editing the DNA template is the Holy Grail. If we could reverse engineer their change agent—"

Frey interjected, "We're not about to go into competition against the Huli jing, Rad. I rather like being alive."

"No, of course not. But what about selling the tech? Anonymously. In the blockchain markets. It would be worth a bloody fortune."

Durand cast a dark look Desai's way. "What the hell are you talking about—selling *it*? Selling what?"

"The technique only, Mr. Durand. Just the technique. A blood sample is all we need."

Frey was nodding to himself. "I will say it makes sense that the Huli jing would be the first to have this. They have more unwilling human test subjects for genetic experimentation than I care to contemplate. They've got hundreds of billions of yuan."

"It is unethical, without question, but think if they accomplished it, Bryan. Think what it would mean."

"I wonder what they're doing with it."

Durand looked closely at Frey. "Will you help me?"

Frey sighed. "I'll need to confirm it first. I'll want to do as Rad suggests and compare your current DNA with the original Durand DNA." He looked to Desai. "You say you have it?"

"Yes. Mr. Durand has some hairs with the root attached."

Frey searched in his bag and came up with a sterile test kit, which he ripped open. "A saliva sample, if you will, Mr. Durand."

"How do I know you'll even help me after you get this sample?"

"Because if I can confirm what Desai says, I'll want to take you to meet some people."

"What people?"

"People with the resources to actually do something about this."

Durand thought for a moment. "A baby lab. You mean a baby lab."

Frey held up his hands for patience. "A few years back I worked with an embryo-editing ring in Thailand—a gang called the Luk Krung.

These days they handle some pretty radical edits. There could still be some trace of this change agent in your cells. Some viral machinery. Something that would clue us in to how the Huli jing did it. Modeling even simple genetic edits for an embryo is computationally intensive. But for an adult living organism? I can't even imagine. Thousands of edits in a complex sequence to thirty-five trillion living cells? We must be talking exascale computing for a significant period of time. The Luk Krung would have the financial resources to access photonic supercomputing clusters for the modeling load—which will be huge."

"And then they'd have it. I'd be spreading this madness even further."

"Don't think for a moment that the Huli jing aren't using it already. Do you want to get back to yourself or not?"

Durand sat for several moments. How could he even contemplate giving this technology to yet another genediting gang? But then he thought about his wife and daughter. Of becoming the man he was once more. What he was about to agree to was outrageous. He closed his eyes and nodded.

"Good. If it makes you feel any better, Mr. Durand, I don't approve much of the Luk Krung, either. But I don't see any other choice—unless you want to go ask the Huli jing."

Durand said nothing.

Frey handed the swab to Durand. "A sample of your saliva, please."

Durand opened his mouth and swiped the swab along the inside of his cheek. He then inserted it into a handheld device Frey held toward him.

"Very good. A full sequence will be finished in four hours or so, and we'll know how much of you is Durand and how much Wyckes."

Durand brooded. "You do realize that this change agent will eventually make it impossible to hold anyone responsible for anything? It will render identity meaningless."

"I know that commanding the tides to cease does not work. That's what I know."

Durand felt ashamed that he had so readily crossed this line. It was something he'd thought he'd never do. But then something else occurred to Durand. He focused his gaze on Frey. "Why are you going with me?"

Desai laughed. "I should think that's obvious, Mr. Durand."

"I thought you were nervous about going into competition with the Huli jing?"

"I'm not competing against the Huli jing—I'm bringing it to the Luk Krung."

"And you really think this Luk Krung is going to cut you in after you hand it over?"

Frey tapped the table impatiently. "I'll negotiate a sizable finder's fee."

"Which you could do without going with me." Durand stared at Frey. "Why are you so intent on coming along?"

Desai frowned after a moment's thought and turned to Frey.

Frey still tapped the table with his fingers. Then he stopped. "Look around you, Mr. Durand. You're not the only person who would like to make some changes. This supposed 'change agent' would finally allow me to address my own condition. I could finally have my achondroplasia corrected—even as an adult. I could become morphologically normative. What I want in exchange for making this introduction to the Luk Krung is to cure my condition. Which is why my presence at any meeting is mandatory. And that's nonnegotiable."

Durand realized that perhaps his and Frey's interests were aligned, after all—regardless of whether the man could be trusted. He again nodded in agreement.

Desai leaned forward. "You'll still request a finder's fee, Bryan, yes? I did bring Mr. Durand to you, after all, at some considerable risk to myself."

Frey cast a look at Desai. "Yes—especially since your risk is not yet over."

"What do you mean?"

"You'll need to figure out how to get Mr. Durand across the Thai border."

Durand shook his head. "I'm not climbing into that goddamn fish again."

Frey laughed. "I won't even ask."

"Mr. Durand, Bruce has very limited range. It wouldn't help."

They both looked to Frey.

Frey shrugged. "Don't look at me. All I send across borders is encrypted data."

Durand gestured. "How are *you* getting to Thailand?"

"Qantas business class. I'm not a wanted man in Thailand. Meet me in Pattaya City, on the Thai coast."

"Pattaya City."

"That's right." Frey jotted something down on a piece of paper. "When you get there, message me at this number—no names. Do not use it more than once. Memorize the number, then destroy it. Hell, recycle it—love Mother Earth. But definitely *do not* keep it on your person. I don't want any connection between you and me until you're safely over the border."

"All right." Durand examined the number. "You write like a doctor."

"I *am* a doctor."

Desai looked concerned. "Smuggling people isn't what I do, Bryan. It took everything I could think of to get Mr. Durand across the Strait."

"Well, if you watch the news, there seem to be tens of millions of undocumented migrants on the move. Spend some money with the right people, and you should be able to get Mr. Durand to Pattaya City. That's like smuggling someone to Las Vegas—they rather *want* you to be there."

"What right people? I don't know *human* traffickers."

"You could get him a fake passport with sufficient investment."

"A false passport is not going to help Mr. Durand. He's all over the news, and they've got three-dimensional scans of his head, face, everything. He can't go through airports or border crossings."

Frey shrugged. "Traffickers it is, then. Ask your smuggler friends. They must know *somebody*. Offer a 100 percent bonus once our friend reaches Thailand safely. That will incentivize whoever takes him to make sure he arrives safely."

"And who will pay for that?"

"Consider it an investment, Rad. After all, I'm the one putting my neck on the line to meet with a criminal element in Thailand."

Desai leaned in. "Perhaps I should go with you as well?"

Frey shook his head. "My contacts are *my* contacts, Rad. Certainly you don't anticipate that I'd cheat you?"

Desai said nothing in reply.

Frey scowled. "What do you know about me?"

Desai considered the question. "That you are a highly talented, undisciplined genetic engineer who consistently overpromises and underdelivers. That you eventually wear out your welcome in whatever country you find yourself, and must eventually flee upset clients."

"But I *do* deliver. Maybe not precisely what the client wanted or when . . . but I deliver."

Desai nodded reluctantly. "Yes. Yes, you do."

"Good. Then you and I will be equal partners in whatever results. Are we agreed?"

With some hesitation Desai finally extended his hand.

They shook on it.

Durand sighed in irritation. "Already dividing the spoils, I see."

"Yes, and after you take advantage of this technology for your personal gain, I'm sure you'll see it declared illegal." Frey leaned back in his chair. "Now for god's sake, get Mr. Durand out of here—and use the rear exit. I've no doubt that the management of this establishment—and possibly others—recognized Mr. Durand on the way in."

Desai shook his head. "I don't think any of them would be foolish enough to betray the Huli jing, Bryan."

"Regardless. Keep him out of sight and get him to Thailand."

Desai grimaced. "I'll figure it out."

Frey raised his absinthe glass. "I will next see you in Pattaya City, Mr. Durand. Safe travels."

Chapter 18

A **pounding noise roused** Durand. He rolled onto his side. He lay on a sofa in a living room that seemed familiar—though it was new to him.

The sound came again. *Boom. Boom-boom.*

Durand looked up to see Mia. She was just a toddler in a purple jumper embroidered with dinosaurs. She stood on a stuffed chair on the far side of the room, pounding a wooden spoon on an African djembe drum that stood as decoration in the corner.

Boom-boom-boom.

Durand rubbed his face, awaking from a nap. "Mia. Honey."

Boom. Boom-boom-boom.

He couldn't help but laugh. "Mia, sweetie. Please stop."

Boom-boom-boom.

Durand's head cleared, and suddenly he realized he wasn't in a living room at all.

Mia was nowhere to be seen. A spartan microtel room surrounded him. He leaned up to see an intimidating stranger's reflection in the mirror on the far wall—just a meter from the foot of his bed.

Reality came rushing back to him. But the pounding sound remained.

Boom-boom-boom.

Durand looked to the microtel room door. Someone was beating on it.

Durand sat up. The dream had left him with devastating homesickness.

He thought about Miyuki and Mia. About his mother. His brother and sister back in Colorado, too. About his friends. His colleagues. What were they doing about his disappearance? He knew the authorities were searching for him, but did they already believe he was dead? He couldn't imagine what that would do to his little girl. Or to his wife.

And how long would it take for someone to find the note he'd left in his flat?

The pounding on the door came again. *Boom-boom-boom.*

Durand glanced up at blackout curtains. He had no idea what time it was—or even what day it was. A glowing red clock face in the darkness told him it was 7:22 something. Morning? Night?

Boom-boom-boom.

Durand took a deep breath. He felt more rested than he had since this had all begun. He noticed daylight under the door and could see the shadow of two feet shifting impatiently. It was morning, then. He must have slept about twelve hours. He wasn't even undressed.

Durand went to the curtain and peered through. Desai was out front preparing to pound on the door again. The man held a plastic bag and a cardboard tray of takeout coffee. Durand opened the door and stepped aside.

Desai entered quickly, locking the door behind him. "*Ko ni lubang pantat betul, lah.* I've been hammering on the door for five minutes."

"I was asleep."

"More like a second coma."

Durand stretched and looked in the mirror. He noticed that the majority of his bruises seemed to have faded in the night.

"Well, you look better, at any rate." Desai peered through the door's peephole warily. Satisfied, he turned and offered a coffee cup and a plastic bag sealed with a strip of raffia. "I bring refreshment."

Durand grabbed the bag, tearing it open. "Excellent. Roti canai. Thank you." He dipped the grilled flaky flatbread into a container of lamb curry that came with it—then paused. "Is this deathless?"

Desai raised an eyebrow. "You're a *degan*? You surprise me, Mr. Durand. But yes, it is cultured lamb."

Durand tucked in and spoke with an overstuffed mouth. "Thank you." He chewed noisily.

"Go slow. Your system might still be in distress."

Durand suddenly realized that the food tasted odd to him. He slowed his chewing.

"What?"

"This doesn't taste right."

"It's from the best mamak stall in Johor, man."

Durand smelled the curry again. "Oh god . . ."

Desai snapped his fingers. "I'll bet your taste buds have changed, too. That must be it."

Durand closed his eyes. "When will this end?"

"Fascinating. You must have the taste buds of this Wyckes fellow. Things you once enjoyed may no longer be palatable to you—or at least they may taste differently."

"Yeah. Fascinating." Durand resumed eating. He was just too hungry. Roti canai was among his favorites, but this simply tasted okay. Even that small pleasure had been robbed from him.

"Arrangements have been made."

"How and where?" Durand opened the coffee lid and scowled at the contents. "This isn't coffee."

"Soya cincau—you Americans call it a 'Michael Jackson,' soy milk with little strands of grass jelly."

"Whatever. Maybe Wyckes will like it . . ." Durand took a sip. To his consternation, he did like it.

"There's an autonomous hire car waiting in the alley out back, to take you north."

"A car? *To Thailand?* That's at least a thousand kilometers."

"It's two thousand to Pattaya City, but the car is just to the state of Kelantan here in Malaysia. There you'll be hidden in a truck by smuggler friends of mine and smuggled over the border."

"I won't get that far. Hire cars have interior cameras. Facial recognition. I won't get out of Johor."

Desai patted him on the back. "This isn't Singapore, Mr. Durand.

The car service is owned by smugglers. This car makes a trip up the coast a couple times a week. There'll be some contraband in the panels, but that's the price of pseudonymous travel."

Still eating, he cast an annoyed look at Desai. "Don't even start with me, Rad."

"Custom plant embryos in cryo. Nothing to be overly concerned about."

"I'm trying to avoid the police, not attract them."

"Smugglers make their living with the *cooperation* of the police. This way you're just another mule among many. Your journey will arouse no suspicion."

Durand considered this. "What did you tell your smuggler friends about me?"

"Only that I've a shipment and an associate willing to go along with it. It saves them the trouble of finding a mule. Empty hire cars on long-distance runs are routinely stolen."

Durand tossed the bag in the trash as he finished the roti canai. "Why not a boat across the Gulf of Thailand like all these refugees? A straight shot."

"The Gulf is risky. And I have no contacts with human traffickers."

"Still, the Malaysian peninsula is crawling with climate refugees. The southern provinces of Thailand are under martial law. Muslim separatists. Bombings. There are military checkpoints. It's not exactly a Sunday drive."

"It's not a *war*. It's just a 'zone of heightened security,' is all. Thai soldiers are looking for terrorists, not smugglers. Which is why they accept bribes. You'll be on the back of a military truck all through Southern Thailand."

Durand contemplated this. "How many days?"

"Two. Three at most."

Durand had to admit that it sounded like a reasonable plan. He stood. "What's in the other bag?"

"Oh . . ." Desai opened the bag he held in his hand and produced a theatrical-quality hairpiece with dramatic sideburns. "I thought it best to alter your appearance. I've a friend who works for a low-budget film studio near here."

Durand went to the mirror and tried on the hairpiece. He turned this way and that. He resembled a Eurasian Clint Eastwood. Desai passed him a false mustache and a container of spirit gum.

"Really? A mustache."

"You want to look as different as possible to casual inspection."

Durand used the spirit gum to affix the mustache and then slipped on the mirror glasses Desai had given him the day before. Looking at his reflection, he now resembled a Bollywood action hero. "Won't fool near-infrared facial recognition systems."

"Of which there are few to zero in rural Malaysia."

"Nor is it likely to fool the police."

"Then don't talk to any."

Stepping out into the morning heat, Desai led Durand around the side of the prefab microtel to an alley where a budget autonomous car was parked. The humidity—even this early—was stifling. A fetid stew of odors emanated from nearby overflowing dumpsters. It was gag-inducing. Crowds of Bangladeshi and Burmese immigrants lucky enough to have found illegal employment walked through the alley on their way to work.

Desai extended his hand to bump bitrings with a preteen kid who was sitting on the car—apparently watching it. With that the kid scurried off. "Here we are."

Durand examined a blue grown-shell chitin car wedged in with a row of other poorly parked vehicles—part of the haphazard pattern of life in Johor. The car was a two-seater—a popular low-budget model called a Shrimp (because the body was grown from the same chitinous material as shrimp shells). Painting them wasn't necessary since they were grown with their shells in many colors. Lightweight. Strong. Eventually biodegradable. This one was blue with a mother-of-pearl iridescence and OLED headlamps.

Desai waved a prepaid credit fob to unlock it, and then handed the fob to Durand, who climbed inside. Glancing around, he saw no one taking any notice of them. But then, almost everyone in the city seemed to be from somewhere else.

Desai handed Durand a new phablet device. "Take this—and give me that old one."

Durand hesitated. "Why?"

"Because I've loaded a substantial amount into a digital wallet on this one. You can access the funds here." He pointed. "For god's sake, secure it with a passkey. I've given you far more money than you'll need just in case anything goes wrong. But I expect to be paid back."

Durand handed over the junkie's phablet and took the new one.

"I can also track that device in a pinch if I need to—although I'm going to avoid that if at all possible. I'm not keen on being linked to you."

Durand nodded.

Desai offered his hand. "I wish you luck in returning to your former self, Mr. Durand."

Durand took Desai's hand and shook it. "I appreciate your help, Rad. I really do."

"If you succeed, remember: we could convert this live editing technology into billions of American dollars. The three of us. Literally *billions*, Mr. Durand. Imagine retiring young to your own compound."

Durand stared coldly for a moment—then smiled tightly. "I'll bear that in mind."

Desai shut the door. He saluted, then merged into the foot traffic passing around the Shrimp.

Durand looked at the vehicle number on the front visor and spoke to the car without taking his eyes off Desai. "Comcar 6362, start current journey."

A synthetic voice with a male Indian accent said in English, *"Commencing journey from . . . Johor Bahru to . . . Endau. Estimated travel time, two hours and nineteen minutes, charged to your Sinco card. Please relax and enjoy your journey. You can request to pull over at any time by announcing 'Unscheduled Stop.' Stops will incur extra charges."*

A digital map appeared on a cheap video sticker screen adhered (slightly crooked) to the car's dashboard. No light field projectors here. The interior was as low-budget as they came.

The car began to roll forward, lightly honking its horn to alert the undocumented workers to make way.

a virtual screen. "I got an alert that said Gino's chopper had arrived." She looked up, businesslike. "He's not with you?"

Durand shook his head.

Frey shrugged casually. "Gino sent us ahead. Told us to wait for him here. I'm sure he'll be along in a day or two."

She sighed in irritation. "He's not answering his phone."

"He was quite busy when we left him. And you are?"

She looked irked but said, "Gardenia."

"Gardenia. What a lovely name."

"I'm with Gino."

"Of course. I'm an old associate of Gino's from back in the '20s."

"I didn't think anyone knew Gino from that long ago. You must have some interesting stories."

"None I can tell, unfortunately."

She nodded. "I was going to take a swim."

"Don't let us stop you."

She shrugged and slipped off her robe, revealing her perfectly toned body in a bikini. She walked toward the water, kicked off her sandals, and dove in.

Frey sighed. "Such a lovely view out here."

Durand finished his drink. "I need to get some rest. You should do the same—after you reach out to your hill tribe." He got up, examining the glass walls on the floor above. "I'm going to find a bedroom."

"Looks like there're plenty." Frey raised his glass again.

Durand followed a wide teakwood staircase upstairs into a long hallway. He wandered from door to door until he found what seemed to be a guest bedroom with a glass wall looking down on the pool area below and the broad sweep of the city lights. It appeared that all the rooms had glass walls. He wondered how people got privacy. Or how they slept in. But he was too tired to think for long. Almost as soon as his head hit the pillow—and a very fine pillow it was—he fell asleep.

Durand awoke suddenly in the middle of the night to commotion. It took him a moment to orient himself, but he finally recalled where he was, and as he looked around in the semidarkness, a screen glowing on the wall pulsated in sync with rock music—a pounding beat.

The text at the base of the pulsating colors read "Iggy Pop— Gardenia." He glanced down at the pool area through the plate glass and could see Vegas's Thai mistress and Frey dancing with reckless abandon, poolside, a champagne bottle in his hand.

Durand put a pillow over his head and rolled back to sleep.

Chapter 31

The dream was always the same. She is six again. Aiyana's mother calls to her in their two-room, windowless mud brick house. Aiyana kneels at the hearth, baking kissra—the thin, fermented bread of her childhood. She bakes on a sheet of tin pulled over the mouth of a cut oil drum glowing with coals. The aroma of the bread tantalizes her. But she responds to the second call of her name, entering the front room to see a man in a crisp white thawb and kaffiyeh made of fine cotton standing in their doorway, not entering, for this would be *haram*—forbidden. Instead, he stands in the rubble-strewn street. Aiyana's mother wears a dark toub wound about her body and her hair and speaks to him quietly. This, too, is a sin, but Aiyana's father never came back from the war—the all-consuming, ever-expanding war that Aiyana cannot understand. She imagines the war as a monster that eats people. People fear it. Men go to fight it and never return. Or they come back mangled.

The man holds a satellite phone. He also wears a glittering gold timepiece on his wrist that is the single most beautiful thing Aiyana has ever seen. A blue SUV, coated in mud, is parked some ways behind him in the lane.

The man says nothing to Aiyana, merely looks her over while Aiyana's mother and brothers stand nearby. Eventually the man nods, and Aiyana's mother leans down to her. Her mother's face is always blurry in the dream. Aiyana can no longer recall her mother's face.

"Go with this man now. Do as he says, and be a good girl."

The man takes Aiyana's hand, and Aiyana looks back again,

bewildered, as she is pulled away, out the door, and her mother's eyes watch her go from the darkness of their hovel. Sadness? Relief? What is the expression on her mother's face? Aiyana would give anything to know now. Maybe that is the reason for the dream.

Her brothers look on, for once not teasing.

But the beautiful timepiece is there, right next to her face, wrapped around the man's thick, hairy wrist. She reaches to touch the watch face, and the man smacks her hand away. She begins to cry.

Inspector Aiyana Marcotte woke from the dream as she always did—crying. She fumbled for the light on the hotel nightstand, and then grabbed the medallion on a silver chain she knew was there. She looked upon the dull bronze medallion beneath the light.

A Saint Anne medal. The patron saint of the childless. She had found it in the envelope of her foster mother's personal things—after her adoptive mother passed away in the hospital.

Marcotte had never known that her foster mother wore it. Not until that day.

How long had her foster mother prayed for a child? How long had Marcotte prayed for a mother? What did it mean that Saint Anne was also revered in Islam? In the Qur'an she was known as Hannah. Different religions but the same prayer.

Marcotte sat up and wiped her face. Collected herself. She looked down at the second medallion she had since added to her foster mother's silver chain.

Saint Peter Claver. The patron saint to slaves. It steadied her. She looked up at the window and the sunlight rising above Bangkok. Then she grabbed her LFP glasses from the charger and put them on.

The newsfeeds were on fire. The story was everywhere. Two hundred and thirty-six dead. Thirty-one of the victims Thai police—among them members of the country's most elite anti-terror unit. Prominent civilians from around the world dead. Children dead. Every member of the Luk Krung dead.

And everywhere in the feeds, not the face of Marcus Wyckes but instead the face of the young suited man the media had dubbed the "Angel of Death." Somehow clinic surveillance camera imagery of the

Huli jing assassin had leaked. The same *thing* Marcotte had fought in the street had its face at the top of every media feed. *His touch meant death . . .*

It wasn't a he. It was an *it*. She remembered its unliving eyes. Headlines screamed that his skin oozed poison.

There was a sharp knock on her door.

She walked wearily to the peephole. Her skin was still raw from the decontamination chemicals and harsh brushes they'd used to scrub off the first layer of her skin. The biohazard team had incinerated her tactical vest. Her clothing. Her head was bald after they'd shaved off every lock of hair. She was clean. Alive.

She peered through the opening and saw Sergeant Michael Yi Ji-chang with several grim-faced Thai men in suits. Detectives, no doubt.

Marcotte closed her robe and opened the door.

Yi nodded. "Morning, Inspector. No doubt you've seen the news."

She nodded back.

"General Prem's been sacked. They want us out of the country by nightfall."

She nodded again.

"I'll come and collect you when you're ready." He waited for a response, but finally shrugged and moved away.

"Sergeant."

Yi turned.

"Wyckes committed this atrocity to stop us. We do not stop. Do you understand? We pursue him. He will go to ground somewhere, and when he does, I want him to hear our hounds on his trail."

Yi nodded, looking relieved, and then headed for the elevators with the Thai detectives close behind.

Chapter 32

Well after dawn Kenneth Durand lay staring at the view of downtown Bangkok through his feet. The glass wall made it seem as though he was lying on a ledge overlooking Bhumibol Bridge with its golden, pointed spires.

What troubled him most was that he hadn't thought of his wife and daughter the moment he awoke. Instead, he'd stared out at the city, just grateful to be alive. What he should have been grateful for was his chance to continue—to keep striving to get back to himself. His growing comfort in this form angered him.

A knock on the bedroom door interrupted his troubled thoughts. The knock was followed immediately by Bryan Frey walking in and jumping up to sit on the edge of the large bed. "Sorry to pester you, but the world has apparently not stopped turning. And there's news you need to see."

Frey made inscrutable gestures above a new bracelet he wore, causing LFP projectors to descend from pods in the ceiling. These began shining content into Durand's retinas. A virtual two-hundred-inch video screen appeared, superimposed before the view of Bangkok. Acoustic beams brought sound.

The screen displayed newsfeeds and audio, all in Thai. But with a gesture Frey converted it to English. Harrowing scrolling headlines rolled past beneath grim-faced news reporters: "Pattaya City Massacre. Over Two Hundred Dead. General Prem Resigns in Disgrace."

Durand sat up. "What the hell . . . ?"

Frey watched the images. "After we escaped. It seems Wyckes wasn't content to let his people fall into the hands of the police. Either that or he'd hoped to eliminate you."

Durand felt a wave of horror sweep over him. "Those children . . ."

Frey muted the video. "Police. Children. The clients. And Mr. Vegas—along with his Luk Krung."

"Jesus . . ." Durand's breathing increased, and he could feel his tattoos surfacing all over him. He sat shirtless before a screen filled with sickening headlines. Headlines he had caused. "We killed them all."

"No. Don't say that." Frey pointed at the screen—at a crystal clear surveillance image that was in heavy rotation on all the feeds: the Angel of Death. "*He* killed them. A man 'dripping in nerve toxins.' That's who we need to talk about." Frey froze the image with a gesture.

Durand frowned at the screen. "Nerve toxins . . . ?"

"You remember Vegas was afraid of Wyckes's right hand—the man he called Otto?"

Durand nodded.

"That little Einstein girl, she cried at the mention of Otto. She called him the Mirror Man. Do you remember her saying that?"

"Yes."

"I thought it was strange for her to use such a mystical name. Especially because she was so brilliant."

"She was still just a child." Durand studied the face of the killer. "I think I've met this man before. In Singapore."

"You *met* the Angel of Death?"

"I'll remember those eyes for the rest of my life. Dead eyes. I recognize some of the face. He's changed, but not entirely." Durand turned to Frey. "This was the man who injected me. I'm certain of it."

Frey pondered something. "It's making more and more sense. He's immune to biotoxins." Frey popped a pill from a half-empty blister pak.

"What are you taking?"

"I printed up a batch of nootropics. Improves brain function. It's making things clearer. Follow me on this . . ." Frey pointed. "This is indeed Wyckes's 'right hand.' Do you get it: *right hand*?"

Durand just stared.

"He's an *enantiomorph*."

Durand kept staring.

"*Mirror life*. That's why he isn't affected by biotoxins. He wouldn't be affected by human viruses or parasites or diseases, either. Because he is the opposite of life."

"I don't understand."

Frey snapped his fingers, searching for words. "Chirality. Handedness. Molecules, like amino and nucleic acids, have a 'handedness'—not literally hands, but orientations of a molecule's atoms. They can be reversed—from left to right, to right to left. They could have the same chemical formula, but be mirror images of each other. And thus have different interactions, even though they are technically the same compounds."

"So you think this man—"

"Is an opposite. *All* complex organisms on earth are comprised of left—or levo—amino acids. Nobody is entirely sure why that is, but that's the way life evolved." Frey pointed at the screen. "I think the Huli jing created an opposite form of life."

"*Why?*"

"That's the question, isn't it?"

Durand looked again at the killer's face. "I can't describe it, but there was something about him that was terrifying. It's like he was alive but shouldn't have been."

Frey nodded to himself, riding the nootropics. "Fascinating. I would have guessed it would be no different from a racemic mixture." He looked up. "Which is a mixture of both left- and right-handed enantiomers." He held up a finger. "But . . . perhaps some aspect of mirror life evokes an evolved revulsion in us—some survival instinct that is repelled by its presence. This 'Otto' . . . antiperson—he would have no connection to any other living thing on earth. He wouldn't even be able to digest normal food."

"It can't have been a coincidence that he was there. He must have followed me."

Frey looked grim once more. "It wasn't a coincidence. Radheya Desai is also dead."

Durand snapped a look at Frey. "Dead?"

"Yes. Gruesomely, too. The news said it was a gang killing. But I think it was Otto looking for you."

Durand lowered his head into his hands. "I've gotten all these people killed."

"No." Frey pointed at the screen. "It is this person—or this antiperson—who's done this. It's Marcus Wyckes who's done this. Not you."

"I caused it to happen."

"You degans are always so willing to accept guilt. You were just trying to survive, Ken."

Durand gestured to the image of Otto on the screen. "He was there because of me. All those people died because he had come there to kill me."

"And what about the police? What were the police doing there?"

"I don't know." Durand lowered his head into his hands again. "I don't know." Durand looked up. "And what does it matter if this man is 'mirror life' or just a killer? All it shows is how twisted the Huli jing are—to create this abomination."

Frey crawled toward Durand across the bed. "Ah, that's where you're wrong, my friend. I think there might be a link between your transformation and this Otto. Look . . ." He poked the trefoil knot tattoo still visible on Durand's arm. "Why is the Huli jing lab symbol a trefoil?"

Durand examined the tattoo. The single looping line.

Frey tapped it. "These are Wyckes's tattoos. Tattoos are personal things. We've been wasting an incredible source of intelligence about Wyckes that's woven right into your skin. Unless he was on a bender when he got these, he didn't choose them by chance."

Durand looked down at his arm again.

Frey jabbed a tattoo. "A trefoil is significant. I don't know why it didn't occur to me before. A trefoil knot is the simplest chiral knot in existence—meaning it is not identical to its mirror image. And DNA trefoils have major implications in intramolecular synapsis of—"

"English. English, please, Bryan."

"Right. That's the nootropics talking." He stood on the bed examining Durand's tattoo array, studying them like a psychic reading a palm. "What

I'm saying is that I think the trefoil holds the key to the change agent's morphology." On Durand's blank look, he explained: "Its structure."

Durand nodded. "Okay."

"But there's more." Frey pointed at the screen. "What do you see on Otto there? On his neck. Do you see it?" He zoomed the image in.

Durand saw a tattoo of a gray-white-and-gold butterfly on the man's neck. There were other tattoos, but the butterfly was most prominent.

"Just like yours, probably not visible unless the blood's up—like yours is now. But . . ." Frey stretched the skin over Durand's butterfly, comparing it to the tattoo on the screen. "He and Wyckes got matching tattoos. Check it out. Same species and everything."

"But that doesn't tell us what it means."

Frey poked him. "Maybe it does. Huli jing—if we had bothered to read up on our mythology—is a shape-shifting mythological being. A mischievous spirit that can—"

"Take any form. Yes, I know. I sat through a briefing on the Huli jing the day I got injected. Interpol thought the name meant Wyckes's organization wanted to remain hidden."

"Clearly the name—and the tattoo—was chosen for its literal meaning." He tapped his finger on Durand's butterfly tattoo again. "And I think this butterfly was as well. What do butterflies undergo?"

"Metamorphosis."

"Right. *Metamorphosis*—changing from a caterpillar into its final form. Do you know something interesting about caterpillars and butterflies that not a lot of people realize?"

"What?"

"A caterpillar and its butterfly have the same genetic sequence." Frey pounded his fist into his hand. "Same exact DNA and completely different forms. How is that possible?"

Durand realized he'd never known that. And it did seem puzzling.

"Epigenetics. Gene expression. Turning genes on and off. That's what happens during the butterfly's metamorphosis. It builds a chrysalis and secretes chemicals that cause it to fall into a comatose state as its body changes."

"Like my coma. After they injected me."

Frey nodded. "I think that's what the Huli jing discovered—not only how to edit DNA, but how to turn genes on and off on demand, not simply write them into the chain. After all, computer code doesn't do anything unless you execute it." He stabbed at Durand's butterfly tattoo. "I think *this* was the butterfly species that helped them figure it out, and why Wyckes and Otto wear it as a tattoo: *Archon apollinus*. The False Apollo."

"What did you just say?"

Frey turned to him. *"Archon apol—"*

"No, the other name."

"False Apollo."

Durand got to his feet and paced. "Christ . . ." He rubbed his hands over his bald, tattooed scalp. "Get rid of his damn face, please."

"Oh. Sorry." With a gesture, the television screen blinked out of existence. Frey watched Durand. "What's up?"

"False Apollo. Is that really this butterfly's name?"

"I checked it this morning. I've been busy. Talk to me."

"I worked on an anti-bioterror team back in the '30s. Naval Intelligence. We were searching for nihilistic terrorist groups. Or brilliant idiots. People who might accidentally or purposely create genetic weapons that could wipe out humanity. Either directly or by crippling our ecosystems."

"So, what about this False Apollo?"

"They briefed all the teams on it. False Apollo. It was the name of a multibillion-dollar illicit biodefense project. It was a big deal. They shut it down."

"It was a *military project*?"

"It was unclear who was running it. Government. Industry. No one knew. It spanned borders."

"What was False Apollo's purpose?"

"To create a universal defense against an extinction-level pathogen."

"In other words: mirror life."

Durand shrugged. "I don't know. Like I said, they shut False Apollo down. I never saw it. Maybe parts of it got out into the world. We were warned to keep a lookout."

"Well, fuck me . . ." Frey pondered the implications. "The name fits. Apollo was the Greek god of music, healing, and light. But he was also the god of plagues." Frey looked up. "So the Huli jing might be remnants of a rogue biodefense project?"

Durand paced. "No wonder they had so many connections. We've got to get moving."

Frey nodded. "Gardenia and I were able to transact some business last night."

Durand gave him an exasperated look. "I'm not interested in your—"

"Not that sort of business. I mean *business*. She was more than a little concerned when she learned of Vegas's demise, and she was eager to exchange the baht we had for biocoin. She might be heading to her home village to lie low for a while."

"Can we trust her?"

"We're going to have to trust her. Vegas trusted her, and she was more than helpful. Look . . ." Frey held up a gleaming piece of obsidian etched with a gold stylized aircraft logo. "She showed me where he kept his credit fobs."

"What is that?" Durand took it.

"A hideously expensive, zero-memory, on-demand autonomous electric jet service—Jet Black. This will bring us a lot closer to Myanmar."

"We won't be able to get near an airport."

"We won't have to. Vertical takeoff and landing. We can use the helipad outside. Costs a goddamned fortune, but it's not our money." He took the credit fob back. "More importantly, I got in touch with my Shan contact last night. They're still alive, and they said they would agree to smuggle us over the border and through the Burmese highlands— although it's going to cost us."

Durand started to get dressed. "How much?"

"Half a million US dollars. Pretty much everything we had."

"How do you know these Shan people of yours aren't going to just kill us?"

"Their payment is contingent on our safe arrival in Naypyidaw. With Gardenia's help, I converted all our cash into a single encrypted wallet, and gave the Shan a down payment of a hundred thousand. They get the balance when we arrive safely."

"They could torture the code out of you."

"They'd have no reason to. They're making the trip anyway, and I've helped them a great deal in the past—which is the only reason Shan938 agreed to take us."

"Shan938—that's the name of your contact?"

"It's the only name I was ever given. I've never met any of them in person."

Durand narrowed his eyes. "How do you know these aren't just criminals? Or scammers?"

"Because they've paid me considerably more than this over the years for genetic editing of their crops. And this account holder had the encryption keys and digital signature to prove they are who they say. You must understand, these Shan are a spiritual people—Buddhists. The central government keeps trying to kill them, and they just want to be left alone. They're not criminals."

"What do they know about us?"

"I told them you and I need to get to the capital of Myanmar, and if the central government knew what we planned on doing there, they'd probably try to kill us."

"And they didn't ask what we'll be doing?"

Frey shook his head.

"You conducted this exchange over an encrypted line, I hope."

"Now I'm insulted. I break the law for a living."

"What route will we be taking?"

"They didn't say what route we'd be taking. Operational security. They'll want to be certain we're not working with the Tatmadaw first, of course. All they gave me was GPS coordinates and a date and time to meet: three o'clock this afternoon."

Durand shot a concerned look Frey's way. "*This* afternoon? That's cutting it close, isn't it? What is that, four hundred miles away?"

"Yes, but we'll have a jet. Shan938 said if we arrive in anything else or with anyone else, we'll be shot out of the sky."

Durand just stared at Frey. "What time did you get up this morning?"

"I didn't sleep . . ." Frey brought up a three-dimensional satellite map of the Thai-Burmese border region, projecting it where the video screen was. The entire glass wall was replaced by an aerial view of hundreds of square miles of jungle-choked mountains and brown, snaking rivers. A yellow dot highlighted a mountain clearing fifteen kilometers from the Burmese border. "That's where they wanted to meet."

Durand pointed at the bracelet Frey was using to control the video screen. "Where'd you get the comm bracelet?"

Frey went into the hallway and came back with a box brimming with dozens of phablets, bracelets, circlets, and LFP glasses. He dumped them on the bed. "Like I said: Tang liked his privacy. These are all prepaid. Bought by surrogates from all over Thailand. He even kept receipts." Frey smirked. "You know what they say: when privacy is criminalized, only criminals will have privacy."

Durand poked through the pile. "I'm not who you think I am, Bryan. I'm no more a fan of total surveillance than you are." He grabbed a pair of LFP glasses and looked back up at the map projected over the glass wall. "These Shan people of yours, you're confident they can smuggle us to the capital?"

"They smuggle everything. The Burmese military has declared foreign biofacturing tools and software illegal. The resistance brings in high-tech equipment, weapons, money."

Durand turned the mountainous map model this way and that. It looked like seriously rugged terrain. "You said the central government deployed deep-maneuver weapons in this region?"

Frey gave him a blank stare.

"Autonomous drones. Robotic weapons."

"Oh, right. Last year. It's a regular arms bazaar out there."

Durand grunted. "Those might be a problem. The worst ones generate their own energy—grow their own algae biofuels from decomposing plant matter. They can remain in the field for months. Sometimes years. Waiting."

"Why am I not surprised you know about this sort of thing?"

"I didn't say I approved of them. I just know about them." He looked back at the map. "Let's summon this Jet Black of yours."

● ● ●

They waited on the patio for nearly an hour, but finally they heard the hissing sound of an approaching jet. The Lilium electric jet was sleeker than the Ehang chopper—predictably black, with wings that extended from the rear of a lozenge-shaped cabin and smaller ducted electric fans up front. A line of dozens more small-ducted fan jets ran the entire length of both wings. Apparently it utilized an array of massively redundant smaller jet engines instead of a few big ones.

The aircraft rose above the railing from below, rotated, and settled with uncanny accuracy in the center of the helipad. Its jets wound down while a voice called out loudly, *"Stand clear. Stand clear. Stand clear."* Red lights flashed.

Once the engines fell silent, the tinted gull-wing doors opened, as did a luggage compartment. *"Call me Jet Black. Welcome."*

Durand watched with some consternation as Frey dragged two large duffel bags across the pavement. He struggled to heave them into the jet's cargo bay. "What's all that?"

"If you're concerned about theft, let me remind you that the former owner was a criminal. So it's already stolen—I'm just moving it."

Durand shook his head and climbed into the passenger compartment. Again a two-seater, it was even more finely appointed than Vegas's fleet of Ehangs. The seats looked to have been handmade with real, organic leather.

Frey followed a moment later. As he sat down, the synthetic voice spoke: *"Aircraft overloaded by twenty-seven kilograms. Please remove at least twenty-seven kilograms of weight."*

"Damnit." Durand got out before Frey could beat him to it. He opened the cargo hatch and pulled out the first duffel bag. It was unwieldy. He unzipped it. "What the hell is in here?"

Durand pulled out what looked like a portable pharmaceutical printer.

Frey came up alongside him. "The Shan could make good use of that. Korean-made. It's high-quality gear, and it'll only be confiscated by the police if it remains here."

Durand pulled out a dozen bottles of expensive-looking liquor, packages of vaping supplies. He tossed them onto the patio, then shoved the half-empty duffel bag back into the cargo compartment.

They both climbed back in and buckled up in frosty silence.

Frey finally said, "That wasn't all for me, you know. There are gift protocols in Asian society that one should try to follow."

"Half a million dollars makes a damn nice gift."

"Say 'Jet Black' and tell me your desired destination."

AR maps and gauges appeared in front of them both. Frey began to manipulate the map to enter destination coordinates.

Durand stopped him. "Don't enter the coordinates now. Plug in a popular destination nearby. A tourist spot would be perfect."

"I've got the GPS coordinates right here."

"If anyone's tracking us, we don't need to give them hours to prepare a reception committee. Give it a destination that isn't going to set off any red flags, and we'll change it at the last minute when we get close."

"I suppose I should listen to a man who spies on people for a living . . ." Frey spoke to the AI. "Jet Black: Fly us to . . . Chiang Mai Airport, please."

"Why do you say 'please' to these things?"

"Because it's polite, that's why."

"They sell that information to advertisers."

"They sell the fact that I'm polite to machines?"

"They sell the fact that you're susceptible to technical animism."

"So what if I am?"

"Tell me that after your machines start to sound wounded if you don't buy something."

The electric duct fans hissed to life, and a synthetic voice spoke: *"Your journey to Chiang Mai International Airport is estimated at two hours and thirteen minutes. Please prepare for liftoff, and feel free to call my name if you need anything while we are en route."*

Chapter 33

The Lilium electric jet was smooth and quiet. They cruised along at three thousand meters altitude going several hundred kilometers per hour. Durand reclined, consumed with his own thoughts, while Frey snored, sound asleep just minutes after takeoff.

Durand watched the mirrored office towers of Bangkok's CBD recede quickly behind them. Before long they soared past the last residential block and golf course and set out over a patchwork of long, rectangular rice fields. Durand could see orange robotic farm machinery in the shallow rice paddies. The wide central plain of Thailand spread out before him, traced by glittering rivers and dotted with golden temples.

Despite his deep concerns over what lay ahead, Durand found himself thinking about how much his daughter, Mia, would have loved this flight. He suddenly felt very homesick—but also relieved to feel that again. He tried to keep his focus on who he was: he was Kenneth Durand. Examining his arms, he was comforted to see that his tattoos had hidden themselves again. They seemed to be appearing more and more lately.

As the Lilium jet traveled north, the rivers multiplied and hillocks appeared in the plains, until green jungle foothills drew in from either side. Mountainous regions were barely visible beyond the humid haze. The occasional gleaming golden pagoda caught the sun's light. Whitewashed stupas and the stepped roofs of temples mixed in with office buildings and shopping malls. The little jet raced northward for hours until around midday a large city came into view ahead. The AR mapping system labeled it Chiang Mai, with cultural markers popping up like mushrooms.

Soft chimes sounded. *"I hope you're enjoying your flight. We've begun our descent to Chiang Mai International Airport autonomous transport terminal, and should be on the ground within ten minutes."*

Durand nudged the snoring Frey as the jet began to descend.

Frey snapped alert. "Yes. What is it?"

"Time to enter your coordinates."

"Chiang Mai already?"

"Yes."

"Damn. I want to bring this seat with us. Let me sleep for just a few more minutes."

Durand elbowed Frey sharply in the ribs. "Up! Key in the coordinates."

Frey sighed and sat up. He manipulated a few invisible objects in his glasses. "Jet Black."

"How can I help you?"

"Substitute new destination."

A larger map appeared before them. *"Surcharges may apply. Where would you like to go?"*

"Travel to these GPS coordinates: 19° 35' 26.18" north latitude and 98° 0' 54.96" east longitude. Desired arrival time: three p.m. local."

"Please wait . . ." After a few moments the onboard systems calculated their path and displayed a map into their retinas. The synthetic voice said, *"Your selected destination lies inside a safety advisory zone. Additional insurance charges will be . . . 400 percent of the standard rate. Do you accept? Please indicate."*

Frey raised an eyebrow. "Just an extra forty-two thousand US dollars in insurance? Why not? I don't think Vegas will mind." He clicked the "Yes" button hovering in midair.

"A rerouting surcharge of 25 percent also applies. Do you accept?"

Frey gritted his teeth and clicked "Yes."

"Thank you. Estimated arrival time at new destination, three p.m. local time. Enjoy your flight."

They curved left, away from Chiang Mai, heading up toward the mountains to the northwest.

The weather was clear as the jet sailed over jungle-filled ravines, waterfalls, and rapids. Treetops raced past the viewports at their feet. And suddenly a golden stupa dome appeared, glittering in the sunlight, but then gone as they raced still upward past more jungle. When they crested the first mountain, a vast terrain of rugged jungle wilderness stretched out before them. Rainstorms were visible in the far distance, with flashes of lightning and dark clouds and shadows, but here it was still clear. Steam rose from various pockets in the dense forests below.

Durand scanned the horizon. It was becoming clear how vast this jungle was.

Frey grimaced. "Why do I get the feeling we're not dressed properly for this?"

Durand looked down at their business casual clothes and loafers. "We'll deal with it."

"At least we'll be the best-dressed people in the resistance."

They soared within fifty meters of the highest ridge. A golden Buddha statue passed below inside a tiled, peaked roof at the summit.

Beyond it the land fell out beneath them. Ahead tall peaks still loomed. Their destination appeared in AR as a glowing green dot, beamed into their eyes. They were going in. The jet's engines decreased.

"Jet Black here. I hope you're enjoying your flight. We're beginning our descent to coordinates 19° 35' 26.18" north latitude and 98° 0' 54.96" east longitude. Please prepare for landing."

The jet glided downward, rocking in minor turbulence.

Frey glanced at the clock. "Look at that: 2:59 p.m. See? That's what I like about machines—precision."

"Tell me that when we're facing killer drones."

The jet rocked a bit more before it entered a sloping valley surrounded on all sides by much higher jungle peaks. They turned, spiraling down toward the only clearing in sight. It was ringed by tangled brush and short, broad-leafed trees. There were no structures or people in sight.

The jet's forward thrusters kicked in, and they went into a hover just above the landing zone. The grass billowed away from the jet wash.

The synthetic voice said, *"There is no standardized landing pad here.*

In order to land do you agree to accept any and all liability?" A "Yes/No" pop-up appeared.

Frey sighed. "Yes." He stabbed at the button.

Another pop-up instantly appeared.

"Do you agree to an additional 800 percent insurance surcharge? Please indicate."

Another "Yes/No" pop-up appeared.

"Jesus, I'm stealing the money, and I still feel like I'm getting robbed."

"Just hit the button."

Frey tapped the "Yes" button.

"Thank you. Please prepare for a potentially rough landing. And in any event, thank you for flying Jet Black."

The jet rotated, hovered a moment more, then gently descended, touching down perfectly on a gently sloped clearing. The jet motors began to wind down immediately.

It was precisely three p.m.

Frey smacked the dashboard. "After all that it was completely safe. What a waste of a hundred thousand dollars."

"Would you prefer we crashed?"

"At least we'd be getting our money's worth."

Durand opened his door, and a wave of heat and humidity hit him. It made Singapore seem pleasant.

They both exited and crunched across flattened cane grass to the front of the Lilium, examining the jungle hilltops all around them.

Frey scowled. "I'm gonna miss that air-conditioning."

They both removed their suit jackets.

There was a deep thrum of insects, the calls of birds and screeching macaques. The din of living things here was relentless. The clearing they stood in obviously had been hacked out of the jungle, because all around them was deep, tangled brush and trees.

"Where are these friends of yours?"

"Observing us, no doubt."

Just then a sound like a large insect approached, expanding into a deep hum. They turned upward to see a purple consumer quadcopter drone hovering ten meters above them. It carried a camera on a gimbal that turned to survey them and then their jet. The drone then descended and hovered a few meters in front of them.

A synthesized male voice emanated from a speaker somewhere on it. *"Dismiss your aircraft."*

Frey looked to Durand.

Durand spoke without emotion. "We're either dead, or we're going to Myanmar. Either way, we don't need the jet."

Frey nodded but spoke to the hovering drone. "I need to get equipment out of the cargo bay first."

A moment of silence.

Then, *"We did not agree to bring your equipment. Just you two."*

"Some of our gear will be useful. You can come and examine it, but let me just pull the bags out first."

The drone said nothing, but instead edged away from the jet. Durand took the initiative and opened the Lilium's cargo bay, pulling out the two duffel bags. "Disregarding their instructions is a bad way to start."

Frey manipulated an AR interface just outside the jet's doorway. "You've been whining about those bags since we left this morning, but you'll end up thanking me."

The Lilium's synthetic voice said, *"Jet Black here. You have opted to cancel your return journey. I want to be sure you understand that this will end your rental, stranding you here. No refund will be granted for your . . . full-day . . . rental. Additional services and emergency pickup will be charged at triple prime-time rates. Do you still wish to cancel your return trip?"*

"Yes." Frey stabbed at an invisible interface with his index finger.

"Let me reconfirm: Do you wish to cancel your return trip, stranding you here and incurring maximum return-flight charges?"

"Yes, goddamnit!" He turned to Durand. "The very last thing I thought I'd be doing in the Burmese jungle is arguing with an AI about surcharges."

"Okay, I've processed your request. You have now canceled your return trip for a total nonrefundable charge of . . . five million, two hundred and forty-three thousand baht. Please stand clear of the aircraft, and thank you for flying Jet Black."

"Yes, and if I ever need to get royally screwed, I'll be sure to call on you."

Durand and Frey stepped back as the duct fans wound up, splaying the grass in every direction and kicking up debris. Moments later, the aircraft lifted into the sky and peeled away to the southeast, quickly climbing toward the ridge.

"I'm surprised it can lift off with so much of our money."

Once it disappeared over the summit, the jungle returned to relative quiet—except for the ever-present thrum of insects and animals.

The small drone returned. The synthesized voice said, *"Follow me."*

Durand grabbed the heavier duffel bag and passed the half-full one to Frey. They followed the drone as it slowly drifted beneath the canopy of jungle, moving along a barely discernible path through the tangled undergrowth.

Almost immediately mosquitoes began eating them alive.

Frey slapped his neck. "Goddamnit! I can't believe I didn't bring bug spray."

Up ahead, the drone had turned around and was waiting in a widened section of the path. Artocarpus trees leaned in from either side, concealing the path from the sky.

As they reached the drone, they both dropped their duffels.

Moments later Durand noticed a squad of a dozen well-camouflaged men slowly move in on them from two directions, emerging from the bush with long guns aimed and ready.

Durand elbowed Frey and raised his hands.

Frey did likewise. "Hello . . ."

The Shan soldiers wore camo bandanas over their faces, though it was possible to see from their eyes that they were brown-skinned—clearly Southeast Asian. They all wore traditional cinched baggy gray-and-pale-blue pants and tunics of homespun cloth, as well as the traditional conical woven bamboo hats known as kups. But along with these they each wore modern camouflaged web harnesses loaded with spare clips, grenades, radios, and other equipment.

Their weapons Durand recognized as aging M4s (or at least M4 knockoffs) with holosights and tactical infrared flashlights—so they probably had night-vision gear somewhere. All of them wore low-slung military packs.

Durand could see no light machine guns with them, so they were probably a fast-moving recon team. Either that or they had overwatch on the ridges above—which on second thought seemed likely.

Only four of the Shan soldiers came directly up to Durand and Frey; the two on either side kept their weapons aimed, while a man in his twenties lowered his bandana and grabbed the drone from midair, stowing it in his pack as soon as its motors cut off. He smiled and spoke English with a slight accent: "Which one of you is Dr. Bryan Frey?"

Frey nodded. "I am."

The man smiled warmly. "So good to finally meet you in person, Doctor." He bowed slightly, putting his hands before his chest in a pyramid, offering a wai greeting.

Frey lowered his arms in relief and wai'd back. "Shan938, I presume?"

"Only partly."

Durand studied the other soldier standing in front—and noticed the eyes above the bandana were clearly female. Her dark eyes met Durand's gaze—and stared back at him with undaunted intensity.

He lowered his gaze and his hands, putting them together before his chest as he bowed lightly to her.

She tugged down her bandana, revealing an attractive woman in her late twenties or early thirties. She did not smile. Instead she gave a cursory bow and barked at the man who'd greeted Frey—who was still smiling.

"My elder sister, Aye Su Win. She commands. I am Thet Ko Lin. Interpreter. The two of us are Shan938. You have been speaking to her through me. I translate her words. She speaks no English."

Frey looked happily surprised. He bowed to her. "Then all these years I've been conversing with you, Nan Win."

"Bo Win," Thet corrected. "'Bo' means 'commander.'"

"Bo Win. My apologies."

She eyed him and spoke rapidly to her brother in the Shan dialect.

"My sister says you did not mention you were a dwarf."

Frey smiled diplomatically. "Tell her I did not think it relevant."

Thet conveyed this to her, and she looked irritated. A moment later she barked back a string of words.

Thet listened and translated as she spoke. "We have a cousin with your condition, and walking long distances can be an issue for him. It was relevant information."

"Well, surely we're not walking all the way to Naypyidaw."

Thet paused before conveying this to his sister. As he did so, all the men erupted in laughter. She did not laugh.

Durand muttered, "Charming the locals as usual."

Frey whispered back, "I would think five hundred thousand US dollars would at least put us on the back of a truck."

She spoke to her brother but looked squarely at Frey—pointing at him menacingly.

Thet smiled and laughed nervously. "So sorry, Dr. Frey, but my sister says if you withhold any more relevant information from her, she will leave you and your friend behind." Thet laughed nervously and bowed again. "So sorry, but my sister does not . . . how do you say . . . fuck around. Do you see?"

Frey nodded grimly. "Yes, Thet. I see."

Win stepped forward and between Durand and Frey, moving them aside to look at the duffel bags on the ground. She muttered something in irritation as she tried to lift one.

Thet translated. "She says you have brought seventy kilos of what, exactly?"

She unzipped the first duffel to find wads of bank-wrapped Thai baht notes.

Frey looked to Durand. "I was going to tell you about those."

"Were you . . ."

She found two automatic pistols—both Sig Sauers, with oak handles. She slid the action back to find that they were loaded and cast a dark eye at Frey.

"Tell your sister that those are intended for much later—after we've parted company and are inside the capital. And even then, only for personal protection."

She confiscated the guns, unloading them with practiced ease and tossing them to one of her men, who caught them and quickly stashed them in his pack.

"Of course, you'll hold on to them for us."

She also tossed the wads of baht notes to another soldier, who caught them and secured them.

Frey kept nodding. "For safekeeping. Good idea."

Durand spoke under his breath. "Please tell me you don't have narcotics in those bags."

"Would you stop with the narcotics? You sound like my mother. I'm not on narcotics. They're nootropics."

Thet motioned for silence. "Is there anything else in these bags my sister should know about?"

Frey sighed, clearly feeling set upon. "Tell her there's a portable multiplex DNA sequencer with reagents and supplies. A pharmaceutical printer with an array of precursors. A lovely hypersonic music system, and various recreational materials intended as gifts for all of you."

Thet listened intently and conveyed this to his sister, who was already going through the final duffel bag—finding the DNA sequencer. She nodded at it appreciatively and spoke to her brother.

"We will purchase this from you. The price can be taken off your travel cost."

Frey stepped forward. "I only need to use it twice, ideally. After that, you may have it. Consider it a gift to the Shan people."

Thet smiled as he conveyed this.

Win studied Frey, and then called out to another soldier sharply.

The man rushed forward, opening his pack to withdraw electronic equipment.

Thet knelt next to Frey. "Do not be alarmed, Dr. Frey. This will only take a few minutes. It is quite painless."

"*What* is quite painless?" Frey tried to move away but soldiers grabbed him by the arms.

Durand raised his hands but stepped forward.

Two guns were immediately aimed at him from a meter away.

Bo Win shouted, and everyone froze.

Durand looked to Thet. "I won't allow you to harm my friend, Thet. Please tell me that's not what's about to happen."

"No." He turned to face Durand. "We have not been introduced. So sorry."

Durand bowed slightly to Thet, peaking his hands. "I am Kenneth Durand."

Thet bowed as well. "Pleased to make your acquaintance, Mr. Durand."

Behind him a soldier placed what looked like an encephalograph cap onto Frey's head. It rather comically resembled a tanker's helmet.

Durand nodded. "Near-infrared."

Thet smiled. "Yes. You've seen this?"

Durand turned to Frey. "Relax, Bryan. They're just going to interrogate you."

"Why would I relax if they're going to *interrogate* me?"

"It's a portable unit—like we used in the Horn of Africa back in the '20s. With suspected insurgents. It uses near-infrared light to penetrate a few inches into the brain and examine blood flow. It's like an fMRI unit, but lower-powered and portable. The software on the handheld unit has algorithms that detect brain activity associated with dissembling."

"You mean lying."

"Yes."

"Then why the hell didn't you just say 'lying'? You world policemen are always using five-dollar words. No wonder there's a deficit."

"I said, relax. It's not going to hurt you. Just don't lie to them. You have nothing to hide, right?"

Frey was getting his breathing under control as they sat him down.

Thet listened as his sister spoke quickly, then turned to Frey. "My sister wants to know if you are a spy for the Tatmadaw or the central Burmese government, Dr. Frey."

Frey sighed again. "No. I am not a spy for the Burmese army or government, or any government. I'm not keen on central government, frankly."

Win looked at the display on a unit being held by the system operator. Satisfied, she asked another question.

Chapter 45

Kenneth Durand awoke strapped to a table. He was racked with pain, and his face and body felt tight with swelling. When he looked around, it was obvious he was back in the Huli jing labs. In a familiar room.

He heard voices and closed his swollen eyes again. Male voices. Angry.

"We could all get killed if you screw this up."

A more familiar voice. "It will take time to figure out how far the change agent got before neutralization. Then I'll need to compute a new edit plan to undo the changes."

"He was your patient. You should have most of his bio-data already."

"The editing process was only under way for a half hour or so."

The familiar voice countered, "The agent triggers many changes early in the process to prepare for metamorphosis. How did he get ahold of an ampoule?"

"That doesn't matter."

A different voice. "This needs to be done now! Do you hear?"

Yet another voice. "If you do not fix this, you will be the first to die. And it won't be quick. I promise you."

"Forgive! Please forgive! I can fix it! It will take time to synthesize a correction. But I promise you—"

"Mr. Wyckes wanted this subject dumped tonight. He should already be on a plane."

"Tonight? That is too soon."

"Just get it done."

Durand heard retreating footsteps.

Then someone approached his table.

Durand opened his eyes. He saw a very nervous lab technician staring at the ground. It was Hanif—the genetic counselor he had seen earlier in the evening. Durand tried to speak—but it was surprisingly difficult. "Hanif . . ."

Hanif's eyes darted away. "Do not speak to me."

"Hanif."

"Do not speak to me. Please." He got busy moving his arms to virtual interfaces.

"Don't."

"I have no choice. They will kill me." He leaned into Durand's field of vision. "And you lied to me."

Durand's somehow even more alien voice croaked, "I'm trying to destroy the Huli jing."

Hanif paused. Then he got busy again. "It's impossible. Just let me be. Have you not done enough already?"

But then Durand noticed Hanif stiffen. He stood up straight and raised his shaking hands.

Bryan Frey's voice came from close by. "Untie him."

Durand looked to the side. "Bryan?"

Hanif cursed in a foreign language and began unbuckling Durand's restraints. "They will kill me. You realize that, don't you?"

Frey walked into view wearing a medical gown and holding a wicked surgical knife. "You're the one who signed up for this, Hanif."

"I did not sign up for anything. They took my passport. I have been a virtual prisoner for four years."

Durand craned his neck toward Frey and spoke through swollen lips. "You son of a bitch, I thought you sold me out."

Hanif took the last strap off Durand's ankle. Durand tried to sit up.

Frey narrowed his eyes. "How is my not wanting to die selling *you* out?"

Durand successfully sat up, but with difficulty. "You said—"

"No, I stand by what I said back there. You must admit it was the rational decision. I thought I might have a chance to save myself. I wasn't going to work for the Huli jing. But getting revised would certainly have helped to start a new life."

Hanif shook his head. "You would never have escaped."

Machine gun fire and explosions rattled the glassware.

"The Shan attack is still under way."

Hanif whispered, "Gentlemen! You are going to get us *all* killed."

Durand examined his hands, which were hideously swollen. So was his body.

Frey gestured toward him. "I barely recognized you when they wheeled you past."

Durand looked at his own reflection in the cabinet glass. The tightness he was feeling in his face wasn't just swelling. The left side of his face looked partly deformed. Asymmetrical. Other parts of his body felt strange or painful as well. Bruises ran down both his arms. "Shit."

Hanif moved about, gathering items from cupboards. "It is nothing that cannot be fixed." He grabbed Durand's swollen hand. "If you help me, I will help you. Please help me get away from here. I, too, have a family. Back in Indonesia. But where can I go? The resistance is throughout the countryside. They would kill me. I cannot leave through the airport or roads, either. I am a prisoner here. Help me."

Frey lowered the surgical knife. "We know people in the resistance. We can get you out."

"I have your change agent, Mr. Durand. It finished while you were away. I can bring it with us." Hanif moved toward refrigerated cabinets and started rifling through them.

Frey shouted, "Get mine as well!"

"I want immunity! For what I've done. I did not do it willingly. Many people here are wishing to bring an end to this madness."

Durand held his deformed arms out. "What did I do to myself?"

"You injected a sheik's bodyguard's DNA, Mr. Durand. It is fixable."

Frey pointed. "Ah. I can see a hint of it. On the left side." He dropped the knife onto a tray and called out after the lab technician, "You'll find my own change agent is being synthesized in the lab next door. The name is Bryan Frey."

Durand jerked his swollen head. "Go with him, Bryan. We can't trust him just yet."

"Oh, right." Frey nodded and grabbed the surgical knife again as he followed the man.

Durand got up from the table and nearly fell. His legs were swollen, and his rib cage felt strange. He could see his blurry reflection in several polished surfaces throughout the lab, and none of them looked good. To make matters stranger, he was still wearing his dinner jacket and torn shirtfront, only parts of which still fit.

The lab side door hissed opened.

Durand felt another presence in the lab now. That same feeling of dread. He closed his swollen eyes in resignation and turned to see Otto standing in the doorway. The full complement of Huli jing tattoos was still displayed darkly against Otto's neck and hands.

Durand glanced down to see no tattoos at all on his own warped skin. It was strangely a relief. He looked up at Otto. "Wyckes lied to you."

Otto approached.

Durand felt the fear building, but he faced those undead eyes. "I know you're alone. I know you've always been alone."

Otto stopped just a foot away.

Durand's swollen, discolored hands trembled. He held them up. "But I know that inside you're a person. Like me."

"Your kind is an abomination."

Durand nodded. "We are. Sometimes we most definitely are." He caught his ragged breath. "But our minds are the same as yours. If nothing else, we can share knowledge."

Otto stared.

"Humanity isn't going extinct, Otto. I'm sorry. Wyckes will never raise your people."

Otto pounded on the bench and got in Durand's swollen face. "A lie!"

"How do you know those embryos even exist?"

"I saw them! He showed them to me."

Durand trembled, but he faced the uncanny visage. Felt Otto's unliving breath upon him.

"Embryos in cryo. Whole mirror life ecosystems. Preserved. Waiting. I am the first of my kind. The first of many."

Durand, still trembling, said, "How long ago did you see them?"

Otto's dead eyes glared.

"I'm guessing years."

Otto said nothing.

"Go and ask Wyckes, Otto. Ask to see them again."

Just then Frey and Hanif returned. Hanif dropped a metal tray and fell to his knees at the sight of Otto.

"Please forgive! Please forgive!"

Frey stood warily. Obviously taken aback. "What's going on?"

Otto's gaze did not waver from Durand.

"Ask Wyckes to show you the mirror life in cryo. He won't be able to. Because after they had the change agent, they didn't need the False Apollo Project anymore. They incinerated everything when they shut it down. They showed us video of the labs. I didn't know what they were destroying until I met you."

Otto's stare faltered and he looked down.

"I'm sorry."

An explosion outside rattled the glassware again.

Otto spoke to the floor. "What color were the walls in those labs?"

Durand contorted his swollen face. "The walls?"

Otto's terrifying eyes got right up to Durand's as he screamed, "The walls, damn you! What color were the walls of the False Apollo labs? If you really saw them, you'd—"

"Blue!" Durand shook in fear to have Otto so close. "They were light blue! The floors, the walls."

Otto's fierce expression faded, and he staggered back.

"I don't know why everything was blue. But it was."

Otto stared at nothing. His voice was calm. "It had to do with filtering reflected light on test samples."

The room was silent for several moments except for gunfire crackling in the distance.

"Leave this place, Mr. Durand." Otto moved toward the door.

Hanif and Frey leaped aside, pressing against the wall as if a grizzly bear were marching past.

Otto stopped in front of them. He pointed at an emergency biohazard station on the wall. "You will want to use biohazard suits. The atmosphere in here is going to become unsuitable for old life."

Chapter 46

Hanif sealed and locked the lab doors behind Otto after he left. "We must depart if Mr. Otto is going to use what I think he's going to use." Hanif broke open the biohazard station and started pulling out the protective gear. He tested the oxygen mask.

Durand struggled to walk as Frey gathered ampoules and vials of reagent.

"We have more than enough here to provide evidence of what they've been doing."

Hanif ran about frantically. "We must leave! I suspect very bad things are about to happen."

It took them nearly ten minutes to gather all their materials and suit up in biohazard gear. Frey's protective suit looked particularly alarming since the arms and legs were mostly empty. At some point a klaxon went off—whooping as biohazard strobes flashed.

Hanif looked at Durand and spoke through his mask: "We must hurry!"

Hanif entered the corridor pushing the wheeled lab table. Both Durand and Frey were piled onto it as if they were corpses. Durand looked out through his visor at the passing hallway.

Hanif shouted through the radio in his gas mask, "Biohazard! Stand back! Biohazard!"

As they moved through the corridors, Durand saw security guards and clients lying motionless here and there. They showed no obvious signs of injury, but they didn't appear to be breathing.

The biohazard strobes still flashed and the alarms wailed. Distant machine gun fire and explosions filled the gaps. Hanif rolled the gurney partly into the elevator, and then pulled a dead body out of the elevator car before trying again.

Durand could hear his own ragged breathing through the mask as the elevator doors closed and they descended to the lobby.

When they got to the ground floor Durand could see through his gas mask that some of the lobby windows had been shot out. There was glass all over the floor. Several soldiers lay dead—blood everywhere. Other soldiers tended to the wounded.

The sounds were all muted through the biohazard gear.

Hanif shouted again, "Biohazard! Stand clear! Stand clear!"

The soldiers kept their distance.

As Hanif reached the portico, there was no longer any valet. Bullet-riddled cars were scattered about, some burning. Frey pulled off his hazmat headgear and waved like mad for Thet somewhere out there in the darkness.

Durand sat up to help, but Frey stopped him. "No offense, Ken, but I don't think Thet will recognize you."

Soon the lights of the Maybach appeared, and Thet nodded toward them as he brought the car to the edge of the drive.

Wyckes stood near the window in his office, watching the attack still under way. The military was driving the insurgents off, but there was something wrong. He could feel it.

When the biohazard alarms went off, he *knew*. And when there was less and less activity on their comm network. Clicking through the surveillance confirmed his fears.

He waited. And prepared.

Soon enough, the double doors to his office opened, and Otto entered, his tattoos visible. "Marcus."

Wyckes stood up from his desk chair. He wore a full biohazard suit with the hood flipped back to reveal his face. His own markings on display.

Otto stopped ten meters away across the wide floor. In the conservatory nearby the butterflies flocked away from him as best they could. But then they dropped, fluttering, to the floor dead.

Wyckes shook his head. "What have you done, Otto?"

Unlike the eyes of everyone else he'd ever known, Otto's eyes were unreadable to Wyckes. They always looked dead. Unfeeling.

"I need to see them, Marcus."

"Who do you need to see, Otto?"

"My kind."

Wyckes hesitated. "There are things you need to understand . . ."

"Do you realize how much I want to not feel this anymore? This world is a *hell* to me. Do you understand?"

"You're upset."

"You told me my time was coming. That old life on earth would end. You told me I would cleanse the world."

"Otto—"

"I'm tired of waiting. It's time to begin."

"Otto—"

"Show them to me!"

Wyckes sighed. "I didn't want you to find out this way."

Otto laughed ruefully and withdrew a flask from his pocket. He unstoppered it and began to pour the liquid over his arms.

"You were meant to be a savior of mankind."

Otto just laughed.

"You were meant to be humanity's last hope."

Otto tossed away the silver flask. "That's what you've been telling me since I was a child." He extended his arms and smiled his uncanny smile. "You were like a father to me—embrace me. For once let me feel your touch . . ." Otto walked toward Wyckes.

Wyckes flipped the hood of his biohazard suit closed—then lifted an automatic pistol from his desk. "Stop."

Otto halted his advance.

"There is what you were meant to be and there is what you are."

"Give me my people."

"I incinerated your 'people' the first chance I got. Once they were no longer necessary, those embryos went into a furnace."

Otto's icy grin faded, and he lowered his arms—for once looking truly wounded. He then curled into a kneeling position in the middle of the floor and hugged himself while rocking gently. A soft groaning sound came from him.

Wyckes lowered his pistol. "You're no longer a child, Otto. Even then I found your terror at this world pathetic."

Otto continued rocking.

"But it's almost over. I want you to know something before the end."

Otto kept rocking back and forth, groaning.

"*You* are the abomination. As a boy, they gave you to me to be destroyed."

Otto kept rocking.

"But I thought I could get some use out of you first."

Otto rocked harder, groaning louder.

"I'll have to burn your body. Do you know why?"

Otto paused.

"Because not even maggots are willing to eat your flesh."

Otto curled up tighter and groaned again.

"You're no longer a child, Otto. Stand up and face your death like a man."

Otto replied softly, "No, I'm not a child." Then, more confidently, "But neither am I a man."

Wyckes noticed the gun muzzle beneath Otto's arm too late. He tried to react, but just then realized how inferior the reflexes of this body were to his original self. It was like moving through water.

He'd barely raised his pistol when a powerful BOOM threw him back into his leather office chair. His gun clattered to the floor.

Wheezing, Wyckes sucked helplessly for air. It felt like a boulder was resting on top of him. He looked down to see a small hole in the chest of the biohazard suit.

Otto approached with an automatic pistol in his hand.

Wyckes had never seen Otto use a gun in his life. He frowned in confusion through his biohazard face mask.

Otto leaned close. "I have always hated all life on earth. Except for you, Marcus." He leaned closer. "But I was wrong about you."

Otto's hand gripped the biohazard face mask as Wyckes still gasped for air. "My kind of life was created once. It can be re-created. I'm sure the information is in the Huli jing cloud somewhere."

Wyckes felt his breath failing. This body he occupied didn't seem to have half the endurance he remembered as a young man. If he could just sit up.

Otto unclipped the biohazard hood. "Now, before you go, I'd like you to feel my touch just once—for old times' sake."

Wyckes sucked vainly for air as he felt a familiar, all-encompassing revulsion consume him.

The last thing he felt was the horrifying touch of Otto's bare hand against his skin as he let out one last, strangled scream.

FOUR MONTHS LATER

Chapter 47

Durand gazed at the sky through the open monastery window. He saw the same line of palms as always. He lay in bed, a ceiling fan circling lazily above him. It was hot, but he'd grown more accustomed to it. Somehow it felt more and more like Singapore each day.

A moment later Hanif entered with a tray and smiled good-naturedly. "It is time, Mr. Durand."

Durand sat up. "What time?"

"By my calculations, all the rewrites should have concluded. I can find no trace of XNA in your bloodstream. I believe you are—as they say—done."

Durand almost didn't know what to feel.

"The acolytes tell me you've been walking in the room. Recovering your balance fast."

Fear gripped Durand—as it had for several weeks now. He saw the flash of a handheld mirror on Hanif's tray. He started shaking his head. "Get that goddamned thing away from me, Hanif."

"Mr. Durand, you must look upon yourself."

"And is that what it's going to be? Myself? You don't even *know* what I look like! How do you know? I can't look in a mirror, Hanif. I can't do it!"

"You want to go home to your family. I know you do."

Durand pressed his palms into his eyes. "God. I just want—"

"Mr. Durand. Have I not cared for you?"

"That's not the point."

"Are you a man of reason?"

Durand breathed deeply, examining his increasingly familiar arms. And seeing no genetic tattoos despite his deep emotion.

"Does one's identity come from within our hearts or our DNA?"

Durand murmured, "Within our hearts."

"And what is DNA?"

"Data."

"Yes. And your current data now matches your original data."

Durand said nothing for several moments.

"I did not have to know what you looked like. I had your original genomic sequence. You are a man of science. Of reason. Are you not?"

"I was. Once."

He felt the handle of the mirror pushed into his hand.

"No." He pushed it away.

"You must take it. Please. Look."

"No."

"Mr. Durand . . ." Hanif grabbed Durand's chin and held the mirror up to his face.

Before Durand realized it, he was gazing upon his reflection.

And it was his own reflection.

He recalled his nose. His eyes.

He sat up, adrenaline surging. He stroked his chin. "My god . . ."

Hanif held up Durand's well-worn family photo from its place on the nightstand. He pointed to the man in the photo. "Do you see yourself?"

Durand felt tears run down his face and he lowered his head. He then took one more look in the mirror. "My god." He threw off the covers and looked again at his body. His familiar runner's body.

He was still bruised, and smaller in stature than he'd recently been used to, but he recalled this form. It felt comfortable to him.

He put the hand mirror back on the tray. "How is Bryan recovering?"

Hanif winced slightly and made a motion with his hand. "I believe he will start to come around soon."

Durand wasn't liking what he'd been hearing about Frey. Hanif was being far too evasive. "Is he at least able to walk?"

Hanif looked away. "He is in the great room on the first floor."

Durand remembered this was where the monks took care of disfigured children—results of Huli jing genetic experimentation.

"I need to go see him." Durand got up unsteadily. "I need to see if I can help him."

With Hanif's assistance, Durand left the room and limped down a long staircase. They could hear children laughing outside.

Durand moved down the tiled hallways of the monastery, and as they passed several of the children's wards, he was surprised by the number of empty beds. "What's happened, Hanif?"

A young Burmese girl raced past Durand, almost toppling him. She was followed by another two girls, one limping but moving fast on a crutch to keep up.

Hanif nodded. "Ask Dr. Frey."

Durand looked up to see Bryan Frey sitting at the bedside of a slightly deformed boy of about four. Frey looked exactly as he had when Durand last saw him—still in the grip of achondroplasia. Still with shortened arms and legs.

Frey's short fingers nonetheless performed a sleight-of-hand magic trick with a marble for the boy—whose own arms were mildly warped. The little boy laughed as Frey again produced the marble from thin air. "There you go. You might actually be able to make use of that soon enough, little man."

"Bryan."

Frey looked up, peering over old-fashioned reading glasses and finally casting a quizzical look Durand's way. "Who are you?"

He should have expected it, of course, but the realization still stunned Durand. Frey did not recognize him. At least not on sight.

Hanif supported Durand. "Bryan, this is Kenneth Durand."

Durand put a hand to his chest. "It's *me*."

Frey removed his reading glasses and sighed. "I'd gotten used to the old you."

Hanif tsk-tsked him and helped Durand to sit down on an empty bed nearby. "This is indeed Mr. Durand. I transformed him myself."

Frey glanced over at the burn scar still on Durand's arm from the drone cowling from all those months ago. It was the one thing that endured. "I'll be damned. So you are you." He looked up at Durand's face. "I'd say you look good, Ken, but . . ." He chuckled. "You look like a cop, man."

Durand examined Frey. "Why are you . . . ?"

Frey glanced down at himself. "Oh. Why am I still me? How nice of you to ask."

"You know what I mean."

"Yes. I suppose I did go through some inconvenience to get myself transformed."

"Just a bit."

Frey pulled a necklace out from his shirtfront. On the end of it was an ampoule filled with a golden liquid. "I might still one day." He looked around at the half-populated children's ward. "But for the moment, I've too much work to do."

Durand looked around the ward as well. The children in sight seemed markedly improved. The rest were gone. "My god . . ."

Frey jumped down off the chair. "Follow me."

Durand realized he'd been hearing the laughter of children more and more over the months. It had happened so slowly that he hadn't noticed, but he didn't recall hearing any laughter here during his first visit.

Hanif helped Durand move along, but Durand finally shrugged him off. "I can walk. I can walk. Thanks, Hanif." He walked shakily alongside Frey.

They moved out onto a wide patio. Below in the yard children were running around, some limping, others moving gracefully. Young monks in saffron robes tried to keep order, laughing as children tossed balls to one another.

Durand felt a moment of clarity. "My god. Look at them. You fixed them."

Frey nodded. "Still a lot of work to do. And more arrive each day."

Hanif stood alongside. "The survivors of the Huli jing are coming here. Dr. Frey helps them."

Durand gazed out at the children. "But not yourself."

"I couldn't very well help them if I was bedridden. There was a great deal to learn. Hanif has been an extraordinary help. And there's no telling how long the Huli jing photonic cloud servers will still be up. They could go down any day."

Durand marveled at the scene. "How did they recover so fast . . . ?"

"Because I didn't need to do massive edits to them. For many it was just a single edit. It took a whole menu of edits to get you back to yourself." He nodded at the children. "But these kids, they already were themselves. They just needed a little tweak to activate key genes." Frey looked back to Durand. "As I said, Hanif has been most helpful."

They moved back inside, walking past monks performing physical therapy with healing children.

Durand looked around in amazement. "And here I thought this change agent was going to make the world a nightmare."

Frey waved him off. "Only for us early adopters. In fact, your kind might soon be out of a job."

"How do you figure?"

"The Treaty on Genetic Modification—soon everything that gets changed will be able to be changed back. Germ line edits won't mean anything. No more threat of superviruses or gene drive weapons wiping us all out. In fact, I think I have a new line of work for you, Ken."

"How kind of you to think of me."

"What do you think of this? Genetic security service. Like a credit monitor—but for DNA. People deposit their original DNA for reference, and you test their DNA periodically to see if it's changed. You'd still get to wear a suit and stick your nose in other people's business."

Durand nodded. "Sounds right up my alley."

They stopped near the gateway to a temple, where a golden Buddha stood.

Frey pointed. "You'll find Thet through there. He's usually here in the afternoons."

"Thet's here?"

"Go pay your respects. I think he would appreciate it."

Durand's face grew serious.

Frey looked away. "I expect we will not meet again, Agent Durand." He turned. "But if we do, hopefully you'll go easy on me." Hanif moved to join him.

Durand called out to Frey, "Bryan, if we meet again, I'd say the world is in big trouble."

Frey laughed, and then he turned a corner, Hanif on his heels.

Durand moved slowly down into the temple, past burning candles and incense. He soon found Thet kneeling, his hands clasped before him. Smoke curling from an incense burner.

Durand waited nearby.

Thet soon looked up and stood.

It occurred again to Durand that he was no longer the same man Thet knew. Not physically. He placed a hand on his chest. "Thet. I am Kenneth Durand. You know me. I'm sorry to disturb you. Dr. Frey said . . ."

Thet nodded. He smiled weakly and approached. "It is very strange to see you . . . Mr. Durand . . . like this. But Buddhist teachings prepare us for such things. Of course you are Mr. Kenneth Durand. It is good for our eyes to meet again."

Durand looked to the incense burner.

Thet gestured. "Praying. For the spirit of my sister, Bo Win."

Durand caught his breath. "I see." He took another, deeper breath. An indescribable sadness came over him. "Thet, I'm sorry. I—"

"No, no, Mr. Durand. She would be happy." He moved to point toward the wall—then cupped his ear.

Durand heard the children playing.

"We all live many lives, Mr. Durand."

Durand nodded again. He bowed a deep wai to Thet.

Chapter 48

Durand stepped down from the jet and into Singapore's familiar humidity. Several vehicles waited nearby on the tarmac of Changi International. He felt a smile come to his face as he saw his wife, Miyuki, release Mia. His daughter ran to him.

She screamed in joy as he picked her up. "Daddy! Daddy!"

He kissed her and hugged her close. Her fragrance brought him back to himself more than anything yet.

Miyuki was half a step behind. She wrapped her arms around him, and he felt the wetness of her tears. They shared a deep kiss and hugged again.

"I was worried I'd never see either of you again."

Miyuki held his gaze. "We thought we'd lost you."

"No. I'm here." He held them tight, then tucked Mia under his arm. She giggled, and he moved at a stagger toward the others waiting for him.

Michael Yi Ji-chang and Claire Belanger closed the distance—Yi with an almost disbelieving grin on his face.

Claire hugged him and gave him a kiss on both cheeks. "We were elated to hear you were safe, Ken. Welcome back. It is a miracle."

Yi pushed aside Durand's handshake and just grabbed him, slapping him on the back. "Holy crap, buddy. You have no idea. You're not going to believe everything that's happened while you've been gone."

"No, probably not. But I gotta tell you, Mike, I just want to go home right now." He kept a tight hold on his daughter, who was still laughing.

Yi nodded. "Of course. You ring me when you're ready."

"I will." Looking up, Durand could see Inspector Aiyana Marcotte standing next to a chauffeured car, waiting for them. An SPF security detail stood close at hand. Durand put his daughter down, and as his family approached, Marcotte opened the passenger door for them.

"Welcome back, Agent Durand." She extended her hand.

He shook it firmly. "Thank you, Inspector."

"When you're back on duty, Sergeant Yi will catch you up on everything we've been doing. You have a good partner there."

"Yeah, I know. Did he tell you about the whole Korean Han thing?" She laughed. "He did."

She leaned over the door as Miyuki and Mia got into the car.

"The Myanmar raids appear to have broken the back of the Huli jing. What we discovered in Naypyidaw was truly shocking. And it all came from an anonymous tip."

Durand looked at her. "Did it remain anonymous?"

Marcotte studied him. "Yes, it did. But someone deserves my thanks."

"Someone would say forget about it."

She nodded.

Durand got into the car.

"It's all over the news, you know—a means for editing the living. They say it will change everything. The Post-Identity World, they're calling it. Police work is about to get harder. I seem to remember Marcus Wyckes was down here warning us about that a few months ago. But somehow he got away."

"I wouldn't know anything about that, Inspector." Durand nodded toward his wife and daughter. "Now, if you'll excuse me."

"One more thing . . ." She leaned down. "We found Marcus Wyckes's body in Naypyidaw."

"Don't be so sure."

She studied Durand's expression. "I'm not. We also still need to find this 'Mirror Man' you mentioned in your report."

Durand gave her an exasperated look.

She nodded. "We'll talk more." Marcotte nodded also to Miyuki and

Mia, then shut the door behind them. She watched the car pull away, police escort lights flashing.

Belanger and Yi came up alongside Marcotte.

Belanger spoke to her without turning. "How do we know that's really Ken Durand?"

Marcotte considered the question. "He passed the debrief. Lie detectors. The family seems to think it's him."

"But how do we *really* know?"

Yi watched the car exit the tarmac. "Give me a day or two. If there's one thing I know how to do, it's push Ken Durand's buttons."

Marcotte let a slight smile escape. "Sounds like a plan."

Chapter 49

The banker tried to contain an odd sense of revulsion at her handsome young client. She spoke with a slight Russian accent. "Will you be staying in London long, Mr. Taylor?"

"I just moved here actually." The young man looked up from signing virtual bank documents with a jade stylus carved with dragons. His lifeless gray eyes fixed on her. He was blond with square-jawed good looks, but somehow his presence was unnerving. "My family's originally from the UK, but I was raised overseas."

"Really?" She wanted this to be over.

"After my ordeal I'd like to be closer to family. It's the most important thing to me—a sense of belonging."

"Yes, of course." A pause. "If you don't mind my asking, what ordeal?"

He stowed the jade stylus in his jacket pocket. "I was kidnapped. Held for months by rebels in Indonesia."

True shock registered on her face. "No. You are joking."

"My parents feared me dead."

They probably wished for it, she thought. "How did it happen?"

"Being the heir to my family's considerable business interests does have its downside."

"And your family paid ransom?"

"I was fortunate enough to escape. It took me months to find a way out."

She wondered how anyone could want him back. "Your parents must be overjoyed."

"It's been a bit rocky actually. The drug the rebels used during the abduction impacted my memory—I've lost parts of my own childhood."

Now she felt bad. Was that what was wrong with him? "How terrible."

"But we will be a family again. I'm certain of it."

"Well, you are safe now, at least. And fortunately, as a man of means, you will be able to enjoy all the finer things that life in the London Trade Zone has to offer." She slid his virtual paperwork into an AR inbox he'd made available. "Is there anything else I can help you with?" She smiled, though it took effort.

"Thank you, no." He stood, and one of his two suited bodyguards winced while helping him with his greatcoat.

She rose as well. "Mr. Taylor, it has been a pleasure. I hope to see you and your family soon. And welcome home." She could not bring herself to extend her hand. She hadn't been able to do it when he came in, either. She was appalled at her rude and illogical behavior. She could not overcome it.

Fortunately he turned away without offering his hand. "Yes." He then departed, her gaze following as his bodyguards took up positions behind him. Dressed in a bespoke suit and greatcoat, he was the very picture of establishment wealth—or an old-world vampire. She couldn't tell which.

As he and his bodyguards exited into the winter chill through security doors onto Lombard Street, he noticed not far ahead a crowd of hundreds of people knotting up around some invisible AR content. The growing mob created a choke point on the already crowded London sidewalk.

He moved away from the autonomous Mercedes waiting for him at the curb and donned designer LFP glasses. He walked toward the crowd, gazing up as an enormous AR public news screen appeared on the side of a bank tower. Audio came in through his earphones as the crowd parted uneasily around him. He looked up to watch breaking news unfold.

INTRODUCTION

What is street harassment?

Two of my favorite activities are going running and traveling. I love it when I can combine them and go for runs while on trips, taking in new views with every step. When I was in my mid-twenties and traveled to Oregon for one of my first business trips, I eagerly went for a run through a Portland suburb as soon as I had time.

After a few miles of peaceful reflection as I ran past green fields and through neighborhoods, I heard an aggressive male voice emanating from behind a line of shrubbery at the edge of a yard, "Hey, girl! Run, girl! Yeah, you BETTER run, girl!" Then in an increasingly aggressive and louder tone of voice, he yelled, "Oh, yeah! Oh, yeah! Oh, yeah!"

Initially, I was shocked and my first instinct was to look around. I couldn't see the owner of the voice, nor could I see anyone else on the street. My shock changed into fear.

1

The BraveHearts group raised awareness about
street harassment in Hawaii.

Street art by Tatyana Fazlalizadeh in New York City, NY.

46. "It's not so nice when someone touches you without permission, is it?"

Christine was at a nightclub with a younger friend in Maynooth, Ireland, when a man groped her friend's breast, then smiled as he walked away.

Her friend froze in shock, but Christine "saw red." She ran after him, matched his pace, and then reached around and grabbed his balls. She said, "He doubled over and I held on as I leaned in and spoke directly into his ear: 'It's not so nice when someone touches you without your permission, is it?'"

She said she walked away and when she turned back, he looked very confused and uncomfortable.

Christine said, "I don't think it was necessarily the right way to handle the situation but there is a part of me that thinks (hopes) the guy never gropes a woman again after my response. And I felt empowered for all the times I've been groped and was too shocked to do anything about it at the time."